FIC   MAN

MANESS, LARRY

STRANGLER

3 weeks

β.

STRANGLER

Other books by Larry Maness

A Once Perfect Place
Nantucket Revenge

STRANGLER

A Jake Eaton Mystery

Larry Maness

LYFORD
Books

FIC
MAN

Library of Congress Cataloging-in-Publication Data

Maness, Larry.
    Strangler : a Jake Eaton mystery / Larry Maness.
        p.   cm.
    ISBN 0-89141-568-8 (hardcover)
    I. Title.
    PS3563.A4655S77   1998
    813'.54—dc21   97-40722
                               CIP

Printed in the United States of America

A12003207082

To Marianne

STRANGLER

Chapter 1

He killed again late in October.

One of the parking attendants at the Sheraton Commander remembered the car turning onto Waterhouse Street at about 2 A.M. The apartment buildings across the way were dark, the city of Cambridge quiet.

The attendant saw the car stopping in the middle of the street. He reported that it wasn't a slow stop, more like a dive with the nose dipping down a time or two. The next thing he saw was the passenger door flying open and a woman jumping out. He didn't see her face. He couldn't recall anything about her. Fact is, he didn't look very hard.

The attendant had spent nights and weekends in the attendant's shack for more than a year, parking cars, listening to the fancy lines men tell women in hopes of getting them into a room and out of their panties. Another female huffing out of a car, slamming the door on a man and his proposition, was nothing new.

But something about this was different. Usually the man licked his wounds and gave up: Not so this Saturday night on Waterhouse Street. That's what caught the attendant's interest. The car squealed its tires, jerking ahead with force enough to slam shut the passenger door. Then, in the middle of the block, the car jerked to a stop again. A man got out—a big man. He passed in front of the light of the car's beams and started running after the woman, who by now was crossing Cambridge Common.

Damn fool, the attendant remembered thinking. A big man like that running after a babe. Once he catches her, he won't be able to do anything. He'll be too tired to get it up.

But the running man was not only big but strong. It was not often that all his strength was required, but when it was, he was never disappointed. In fact, it amused him to think of all the good that had come from what his family called his "wasted" life. But he hadn't wasted anything. He had worked hard transforming his muscles into brute force. Weeks ago, he used that force to escape. Now he would use it to make certain that his present run of bad luck did not get any worse.

The big man moved quickly toward the frightened woman. Somewhere a nerve throbbed in the side of his head, a pounding distraction that he willed away. The woman was the important thing, not some wretched pain.

He pulled the brim of his gray felt hat lower on his head as he ran. His overcoat flew open as he sped past signs warning that bicyclists must walk their bikes, that sleeping on the grass was prohibited, that dogs must remain on leashes.

Idle threats, the man thought. His threats were never idle. He almost said it out loud as the woman faltered a few yards ahead.

She was breathing in short, frightened gasps as he bent down and grasped her face in both hands. His thumbs stretched the skin on her cheeks; his fingers dug into the back of her neck, almost prying her eyes open.

The woman dug her heels into the grass, trying to push herself away, but the man held her down easily.

"Last chance, love." His voice poured out like heavy, slick oil. "Where is it?"

She tried to shake her head, but his grip was a vice holding her in place. "I . . . I don't know," she said. "Let me go!"

With a finger, he traced a line of perspiration that formed in the dent of her throat. "A name," he said menacingly. "Tell me."

She gulped desperately, trying hard to swallow. "Promise you'll let me go?"

The big man threw off his coat, then straddled her. "Promise," he said with the icy calm of the lawless. "The name," he repeated, waiting.

Later that morning, after the police had finished questioning the attendant, he was on all the morning news shows, telling Boston television audiences what little he knew about the thirty-five-year-old woman found raped and strangled on Cambridge Common.

The Montrose Spa is one of those quirky little stores that makes a neighborhood. On the street are racks of cut flowers, $2.50 a bunch. If you don't want flowers, you can sit out front at one of the white plastic tables and watch a morning unfold in Cambridge.

Inside, the line for morning papers and strong coffee stops at the counter manned by owners Carmine and Rosie Montego. Carmine is short and wiry. Rosie is short and dieting. She is the neighborhood's self-appointed tester of all diet fads, reporting daily progress every morning at 7 A.M. Today marks the tenth day she's eaten nothing but cabbage—in soup, in a sandwich, in a salad. The progress report isn't very good: only two pounds down, fifteen to go.

"Is terrible," she said, lips pinched in a frown. "I don't wanna see no more cabbages."

Carmine's round head bobbed approval as private detective Jake Eaton stepped gingerly to the counter, a physical reminder that not every man starts the day firing on all cylinders. The evidence of too little sleep and too much drink was written all over him.

Jake had dragged himself out of bed fifteen minutes earlier. He had pulled on the faded green sweats that lay crumpled beside the bed, then headed down the stairs of his apartment, with Watson, scampering after him. Jake's black lab, mixed-breed sidekick showed too much exuberance for Jake's early morning fog. After his morning run, Watson waited outside the Montrose Spa while Jake got his daily coffee and neighborhood news fix.

"Eh, Jake. How you doin' this fine mornin'?"

Carmine's mornings were always fine. Jake wondered how he managed that.

"Not bad, Carmine," Jake said. "Not too bad."

"Never bad when you're alive." It was Rosie's turn. "All I think of the past few days is how terrible that was. And right around the corner."

Jake listened blankly. He took an early edition of the *Boston Globe* from the news rack. The flashy tabloid *The Herald* was stacked beside it. Jake's head hurt too much for flash.

Carmine read Jake's distant look, bothered by the possibility. "You don' watch the news, Jake? Everybody watch the news."

"Been out of town," Jake admitted. "And last night was a late one," he said, explaining that the love of his life, Gloria Gorham, had just bought a town house in Boston's fashionable Back Bay. She was restoring it to the grandeur it once had before being chopped into condos. They had spent most of the brisk fall evening drinking champagne on her roof deck. They hadn't planned on going outside, but the first day of demolition had filled the air inside with a mixture of dirt and plaster dust.

"It was all over the news," Rosie said. "Three days ago, somebody kilt some lady on the Common."

Carmine surmised that Jake wasn't an avid TV fan. "You got a television, Jake?"

"I do." Jake pulled out the exact change, wondering how long it had been since he'd turned on his TV. A month, maybe. Even then, it had been a mistake. Some movie he'd been encouraged to see had been so badly hacked to accommodate the commercials that he'd turned it off. "I just never watch it," he said, stepping aside for the next patron.

Watson sprang to his feet and shook with joy when Jake stepped into the bright morning sun. They turned left down Massachusetts Avenue and ambled toward Martin Street, where Jake lived on the fourth floor of a brick apartment building. He turned down the walkway and opened the heavy wooden front door onto a man looking as haggard as Jake felt.

The man was Bruce Drummond, six feet five inches of no-nonsense newspaperman. Bruce was just past sixty with a head full of unmanageable white hair. He took his finger off the apartment buzzer. "Afraid I was going to have to get your ass out of bed," he snapped. He stepped aside for Watson, trying to control his fear of dogs.

"Good morning to you too, Drum," Jake said.

"Hell, it is. Got any coffee?"

Jake handed Drummond his paper cup from the Montose Spa, then unlocked the inner door. Watson raced up the stairs as the two men trudged behind. Halfway to the top, Jake said, "It's a little early for social calls, Drum."

Drummond was breathing hard. "You need an elevator," he said, hating every step while keeping an eye on Watson. Drummond tolerated Watson as long as the mutt kept his distance.

"An elevator would be nice, among other things," Jake said, thinking that peace and quiet with his morning paper and coffee were at the top of the list. The last thing he wanted was a visit from an aggressive newspaper reporter who thought that every story he ever filed should be nominated for the Pulitzer prize.

Once inside, Drummond went directly to Jake's office and sat in the red leather winged-back chair across from the mahogany desk. He took the lid off the paper cup and sipped the hot coffee as Jake looked on, imagining how good it would taste.

Drummond caught the look. He lifted the cup in Jake's direction. "Want a sip?"

Jake tossed the *Globe* on the desk. "I'll get some later," he said, pulling out the chair from behind the desk and sitting. "What's this all about, Drum?"

"I want to hire you," Drummond said, his blue eyes intense.

Jake settled back in his seat. "To do what?"

"What you do best. I want you to investigate something for me. You probably know about it already," he acknowledged. "You been reading the papers?"

"Nope," Jake answered, explaining that he and Gloria had just sailed *Gamecock,* her forty-eight-foot wooden sloop, back from a few days on Nantucket. "Just got in yesterday morning."

"Doesn't matter," Drummond said, pointing to the *Globe.* "You won't get anything from that rag. Too damned upper crust. *The Herald* tells it straight."

"So you've been saying for years," Jake reminded him. "Now, why do you want my services?"

"I want you to investigate a murder."

Murder always got Jake's attention, early morning or otherwise. "Whose?" he asked.

"Ruth Hill's," Drummond said.

"Who's Ruth Hill?" Jake asked as Watson popped his head in the office before going back to the kitchen for more breakfast.

"The woman raped and strangled on the Common," Drummond

answered. "You must have been away at the time. You couldn't have ignored it if you'd wanted to."

Ah, that woman, Jake thought, remembering Rosie behind her counter talking about the lady "kilt" in the neighborhood three days ago.

"She was a friend of mine," Drummond added, letting Jake fill in what that meant. "She was a sweet kid, one of those research types. Very bright, into computers and all that. We met when she was hired to put the *Herald*'s records and files on-line. When she finished, she moved on. She had a degree from Harvard but was just sort of floating around, looking for the right spot to land. I hadn't seen her for a couple of years; then a few months ago, she came back to the paper to do a little research in the files."

Jake asked what she was looking into.

Drummond shrugged, as if to deflect the question. "I don't know," he said, convincing Jake that he did know.

"You might be one hell of a reporter, Drum, but you're a damn poor liar. Want to start over?"

Drummond's glare was steely. "You wouldn't believe me anyway," he said.

Jake didn't like the change in his friend's eyes. "Try me."

Drummond shifted uncomfortably in his seat. "It's not that simple," he admitted. "A source is involved."

"Aren't they always?" Jake asked, knowing full well the double edge that sources can be.

"Not like this," Drummond insisted. "This is different, Jake. I've never been involved in anything like it."

Drummond's excitement was such that Jake asked the obvious. "Sounds like you're in love again. Who is she?"

Drummond's expression soured. "Come on, Jake. I'm serious."

"Sorry," Jake said, meaning it. "Just trying to get you to open up. You've never been involved in anything like what?"

"The biggest story I've ever locked onto." Drummond scrunched forward, newly energized. "Listen, Jake, I'm here because of the murder of a friend of mine, but that's not the half of what I'm looking into on my own. What I'm working on is way beyond that. Way beyond."

"How so?" Jake asked, his curiosity kicking in.

Drummond shook his head. "Listen to this first: Cambridge PD isn't running the Hill investigation," Drummond said, his voice ominous. "You tell me, Jake. Why would any police force with jurisdiction over a gruesome murder in its own backyard hand the case over to Boston PD?"

"Boston?" Jake repeated, as if saying it himself would give it meaning. "Cambridge wouldn't give the time of day to Boston," he said.

"Right you are. Not when a murder-rape falls in their lap," Drummond added, his eyes tightening on Jake. "Reporters live to write about crimes like this, and cops live to solve them. Cambridge wouldn't give up this case unless someone pulled some strings."

"Why would anyone do that?" Jake asked, then answered his own question. "If Ruth Hill was into something big, it might make sense. Is that what got her killed, Drum? Was she working on one of those top-secret Harvard research projects?"

"Research might have had something to do with it," Drummond said evasively.

"Might have?" Jake pressed. "What aren't you saying, Drummond?"

"Just that Ruth Hill's only a small part in this, Jake. The thread winds way back. More than that I'd rather not say."

"And you expect me to run with that?" Jake said, shaking his head. "Sorry."

Drummond leaned back in his chair. "Come on, Jake. It's not like I pulled your name out of the phone book. Cut me some slack on this one."

"Can't do it, Drum. I don't go poking around in the dark when I don't know where I'm going. It's not good for business when your business is staying alive."

Drummond let out a breath with the sound of a man who knew there was no point in arguing. "You've got a hard head, Jake. Anyone ever tell you that?"

"Often," Jake admitted. "It comes in handy sometimes. Now, about Ruth Hill. What more can you tell me?"

"Not much. At about two in the morning, a parking attendant saw her run from a car over on Waterhouse Street. A man ran after her. The attendant chalked it up to the lady turning down a proposition."

Jake clasped his hands behind his head. He looked up at the ceiling, contemplating a spot as Drummond explained that Ruth had recently started a new job at Harvard University.

"Doing what?" Jake asked.

Drummond removed a piece of paper from his shirt pocket. "I knew you'd want details," he said, unfolding the paper and handing it to Jake. "I jotted down her office number, home address, things like that. Ruth was a technical assistant in Harvard's Psychology Department. She was temporarily assigned to type dissertation drafts for Vicki Shaw, a psychology graduate student."

Jake looked back at Drummond. "A secretary?" he asked.

Drummond shrugged. "There's a little more to it than that," he said.

"I'd say a lot more if connections through her job got her killed."

"Is that where you're going to start? Harvard?"

"I don't think so," Jake told his friend. "First, I think I'll check into what interest Boston PD has in any of this."

"Then you'll take the case?" Drummond asked, sounding relieved.

Jake nodded. "I'll look into it," he said. "My guess is it's one of two things. One is that Boston is doing nothing more than offering a helping hand to another police department."

"And the other is?" Drummond asked.

"The other is that you're not telling me what you know." Jake let the thought hang. "Care to give it one more chance, Drum? Care to speak up?"

Drummond stared silently at his paper cup before taking a slow sip. "Good coffee, Jake," he said finally. "Thanks."

"I'll add it to my bill," Jake said, wondering what he was getting into.

Chapter 2

Jake showered and put on a clean pair of chinos and a maroon turtleneck. He took the shoulder holster from his coatrack and strapped on his .38. He pulled on a brown tweed sports coat, opened the door for Watson, then followed him out into the early morning flow of Cambridge bicyclers, joggers, and dog walkers.

If it weren't for the Smith & Wesson at his side, Jake could have passed for a Harvard professor. At six feet tall with thinning brown hair atop a square yet handsome, mustached face, he was a private detective on his way to buy Cambridge police Sergeant Frank Cowen a cup of coffee.

When Jake called with the invitation, Frank was just going off the graveyard shift. He agreed to meet at the Dunkin' Donuts in Porter Square, a five-minute walk from Martin Street. Watson curled up outside the front door as Jake went inside. The counter was nearly full, but Jake found Sergeant Cowen sitting at the far end munching on a honeydew.

"Coffee," Jake told the eager waitress. "Black. No sugar. How 'bout you, Frank?"

The sergeant shook his large, round head, the last of the donut clamped between his sugar-coated fingers. "Nothing else," he said. "I'm finishing this, then going home for a few hours' sleep. I'm coaching soccer nowadays, Jake. Eight, nine, and ten year olds."

Jake tried to imagine his fat, squat friend pacing the sidelines, shouting orders and encouragement toward a field of scrambling children. It was an image that didn't quite fit the man Jake had known for years, first as a neighbor in his apartment complex before rents shot up and forced Frank out, then as a Cambridge police sergeant. It is said that Frank is so attuned to the city that he knows most rumors before they get started.

"You?" Jake said. "I never figured you had the patience to be around kids."

"I don't," Frank admitted unfazed. "Like always, there's a lady involved. She's got a kid who fancies himself a goalie. The previous soccer coach took a second job, so I stepped in. Men do crazy things for women, Jake. Which reminds me, I saw your picture in the paper a few weeks back. You and that lady friend. What's her name?"

"Gloria."

Frank stuffed the remains of the donut in his mouth, nodding. "That's the one. I figured with your line of work I'd be reading your obituary, then of all places you show up in the society pages," Frank said, looking amazed.

Jake grimaced. He had hoped that no one he knew would see him pictured arm in arm with Gloria and a few hundred others as they kicked off one of Boston's most revered traditions, opening night at the Boston Symphony.

"Gloria's new hobby is introducing me to high society," Jake said.

"Trying to grind off your rough edges?"

"Yeah." Jake laughed. "And trying to improve my dress. Suits, ties, wing-tip shoes." Jake pulled on the collar of his turtleneck. "These are a no-no."

"That's why I remembered the picture." Frank broke into a wide grin. "There you were in a sports jacket and a turtleneck surrounded by all those bow ties and tails. Bold move, Jake," he said, brushing fallen crumbs from his blue uniform.

"Not as bold as what that guy pulled on the Common the other night," Jake said, shifting the subject to business. "D'you know anything about that, Frank?"

"So that's what this is about," Frank said as the waitress brought Jake's coffee. "Yeah, I know about Ruth Hill, and bold ain't the half of it."

Jake gratefully swallowed the hot black java. "What can you tell me?" he asked.

"Not much to tell. A secretary jumped out of some guy's car, he went after her, and that was that."

"You make it sound pretty simple."

Frank wiped his hands with a napkin and tossed it on the plate in front of him. "It doesn't matter how I make it sound," he said, clearly miffed. "Cambridge has been brushed aside. We're not working the case."

"So I heard."

"What did you hear?"

Jake managed another sip, enjoying the tasty heat. "I heard that Cambridge gave up jurisdiction."

"Gave up?" Frank's voice jumped a notch. "You only give up something when you have a choice. This wasn't anything like that. Orders came from the top. Boston was handling it. Period."

Jake looked over curiously. "What happened?"

The sergeant shook his tired head. "Who the hell knows? The 'official' word is that Boston had an 'ongoing.'"

"Into what?"

"Ruth Hill."

"A secretary at Harvard?" Jake asked, surprised. "Come on, Frank. What was she doing, stealing pencils?"

"Officially, I have no idea."

"Unofficially?" Jake pried.

Frank didn't hesitate. "Word is Boston is working overtime to cover its tracks."

Jake read between the lines. "Are you talking cover-up?" he asked.

Frank nodded grimly. "That's what I hear."

Hunting for a connection, Jake asked about Ruth Hill and what part she might have played.

"You'll have to ask Detective Lieutenant Dane, Boston Homicide, about that," Frank said dryly.

Jake perked up. "Tommy Dane?"

"Yeah. You know him?"

"I do."

"He's the one to talk to, but I wouldn't hold my breath. Lips are tight on this one."

"Even yours, Frank? You know what goes on around here better than most. What was Ruth Hill into that makes Boston so interested in her death?"

Jake could see the uncertainty cloud his friend's expression. "I don't have a clue," he finally said. "Before Boston stepped in, we ran the normal checks on her and came up with nothing. Not even a parking ticket."

"Maybe her death was random," Jake said. "Wrong time, wrong place."

"Not a chance. Boston was all over this one too fast. It was like that—" Frank snapped his fingers. "They swooped down the minute the woman stopped breathing."

Jake sipped more coffee, thinking how Drummond had said the thread unwinds way back. "Could Hill's death have had anything to do with another case?" Jake asked. "A murder, maybe?"

"You mean Churchwell?" Frank said as if he'd been toying with the same idea. "Don't think so."

A prickle danced along Jake's spine as he gave Frank a long, hard look. "Who's Churchwell?" he asked.

Frank sat up straight. "What are you on, Jake, a fishing expedition? Lori Churchwell's the woman over in Boston found dead a month or so ago. The papers ran the normal stuff until Boston stopped talking. The story dropped from the pages. You should pay more attention," Frank suggested.

Maybe I should, Jake thought. He asked how Churchwell died.

"She was strangled," Frank answered.

"And raped?" Jake asked.

"That was the word. Don't really know for sure. Like I said, Boston wasn't talking," Frank said glumly. "Or, I should say, Dane wasn't talking. It's his case."

"Interesting," Jake said, thinking it was a hell of a lot more than that. "What's going on, Frank? Any ideas?"

Again Frank shook his head. "Nothing certain. But I hear that all hell could break loose if Boston PD doesn't get its act together. And fast."

"Boston must know something you don't," Jake said.

"I'm sure they do. But, like I told you, if you want to find out what it is, ask Dane. He paid a courtesy call this morning before heading over to Ruth Hill's place. He's finishing up there this morning. Know where it is?"

"I do."

"Try him there. And, Jake, if you find out anything, let me know. In all my years of being a cop, I've never experienced a stunt like this. It leaves a bad taste, you know? Boston's acting like an uninvited big brother. Cambridge PD could've handled this case. Not having the chance rubs the wrong way. Tell Dane that for me. We're just as good as Boston. Tell him that, too."

"I'll tell him," Jake said, tossing a couple of bucks on the tabletop. "Thanks, Frank. And good luck with the soccer."

"Yeah, right. Maybe I'll wind up in the newspaper, just like you. 'Coach Cowen finally wins a game.'" Frank shook his head. "What we do for women, eh, Jake?"

Jake stood and slapped his friend knowingly on the back.

"It's what they do for us, Frank."

"And that is?"

"They put up with us."

Chapter 3

Ruth Hill had lived in North Cambridge on a street lined with wood-framed triple-deckers. Jake noticed, as he turned right off Ringe Avenue onto Haskell Street, that most of the houses needed repairs and paint. The only one in the two hundred block that didn't was the house where Ruth Hill had lived.

An unmarked police car was at the curb, its trunk up. Jake swung around the Boston blue-and-white and parked his old Saab in the drive next to it. He let Watson out to romp in the red and gold leaves that make New England Octobers famous, then climbed the wooden stairs to the front porch. The screen door was unlatched.

Jake stepped inside the vestibule and knocked on the door to the right. In seconds, Detective Lieutenant Tommy Dane—five feet nine inches tall, weighing one hundred and thirty pounds dressed and wet—was at the door. Dane was wiry and rabbitlike with a two-pack-a-day smoker's voice too low and heavy for his slight build.

His shoulders drooped slightly when he saw Jake, as if Jake represented an additional burden. "What do you want?" Dane asked.

"Not going to invite me in?" Jake cracked a smile, waiting.

Dane took a step back. "How'd you know I was here?" he asked. Behind him two uniformed officers packed loose papers from a desk into cardboard boxes with boring precision. Jake thought they looked like thieves making off with someone else's money.

When they finished, one of the officers turned to Dane. "That about does it, Lieutenant," he said.

Dane nodded approval. "Good work," he said, pointing. "Take that to Commander Hoenig's office. Put it with the rest."

The officers each grabbed a box and left. Dane closed the door behind them and turned back to Jake. "How'd you know I was here?" he asked again.

"It's my job to know things, Tommy," Jake said, looking around the simply furnished living room of the first-floor apartment. Ruth Hill's study occupied what should have been a dining room. A computer sat on the now stripped-clean desk. "What's in the boxes?" Jake asked.

"Nothing important," Dane said, turning away.

"Wasting Commander Hoenig's time with boxes of the unimportant?" Jake wagged a finger in mock reproach. "Hoenig will have your head on a platter."

"Just because he tried that with you."

"And failed," Jake reminded him. Still, Ronald Hoenig was a bitter memory of professional dislike. "What's in the boxes, Tommy?" Jake asked again.

Dane took a cigarette from his shirt pocket, lit it, and pulled in a deep drag. "It's not your business, Jake," he said. "Not that I'm not happy to see you. Don't get me wrong. I am. How long's it been?"

"Couple of months," Jake said, aware that Tommy was shifting gears from cold and distant to warm and friendly.

"Too damn long." Dane's head bobbed as if he'd spoken a solemn truth. "Really, Jake. Too damn long. Remember when we used to get together all the time?"

Jake did. It was Dane more than anyone else who'd helped Jake right himself after his wife left him for another man. Dane himself had gone through the same sinking steps toward divorce and had taken on the mantle of resident expert on holy matrimony. Jake shook his head at the memory.

He and Dane had sat up for hours, knocking back a few too many, philosophizing about women and what made them go bad. It was heady stuff, with enough twists and turns in the thinking always to put the blame on the women. How could any woman screw up so badly? How could she walk out on a guy like Jake Eaton or Tommy Dane? There were a thousand answers to those questions, and it seemed to Jake that he and Dane had spent a thousand hours answering them.

"We should get together again soon," Dane added with a politeness designed to conceal.

Jake wasn't fooled but agreed. "How about tonight?" he pressed. "We can talk about Ruth Hill and Boston's interest in her."

Dane feigned a smile as his mood veered abruptly. "Nothing to talk about," he said.

"That's not the way I heard it," Jake said.

"Oh?" The admission caught Dane by surprise. "Since when are you privileged to internal police matters?"

"Internal?" Jake repeated, trying to figure out what he'd missed. "Quite a twist, isn't it, Tommy? Boston takes over a murder out of jurisdiction and calls it internal. What gives?"

"Obviously not you," Dane said flatly. "You should learn to relax a little, Jake. Give it a rest."

"Can't afford to in my line of work," Jake said, stepping to the bay window. He parted the curtain and looked out to the front yard. Watson was curled up on a pile of leaves soaking up the sun, waiting. "What's Ruth Hill have to do with any of this?" Jake asked.

"Nothing," Dane answered.

Jake heard the lack of conviction. "Come on, Tommy," he urged, turning back to his old friend.

Dane took another drag on his unfiltered Camel, then said as gray smoke furled into the air, "Did somebody hire you to check into this?"

"You know me, Tommy. Watson has expensive tastes."

Dane was in no mood for games. "Do your client a favor, Jake. Tell him or her not to waste money on this. Nothing will come of it."

"Because you have it under control," Jake said, completing the thought.

"That's right," Dane said. "Because I have everything under control."

Under normal circumstances, Jake would have been likely to believe his old friend. What little he knew so far indicated that nothing about this case was normal.

"I'll need a little more than that, Tommy." When he got nothing, he said, "From what I gather, Ruth Hill was clean. She'd never gotten so much as a parking ticket."

Dane inhaled the last of his cigarette, then stepped to the fire-place. He rubbed the butt against the top of an andiron, buying time.

Jake continued. "I also heard that Hill's murder might be connected to something else. Another murder, maybe?"

Dane turned back to Jake, not taking the bait. "I don't care what you heard, Jake," he said in a tone almost fatherly. "The fact is, not every woman is the girl next door. Miss Hill may have kept up appearances to look like everybody's sister, but she was far from it. She'd been around the block, all right? She'd been around it more than once. The way I see it, she misjudged one of her male friends. Things got out of hand, and he killed her."

Jake's thoughts went to the papers carried out in boxes. "She kept records?" he asked. "Boxes full of client's names?"

"I don't want to comment on that," Dane said, folding his arms across his chest, resisting the urge to light another smoke. "I will say that this investigation is sensitive, Jake. *Very* sensitive. Boston is making certain that reputations aren't ruined while we find the killer. Satisfied?"

Jake raised his eyebrows a fraction, reading between the lines. What he read spelled someone with enough money and power to warrant special treatment. An internal investigation to keep things quiet meant one thing: the money and power belonged to a cop.

Jake's expression soured. "It's not like you to get involved in something like this, Tommy," Jake said.

Dane bristled. "What I'm involved in is capturing the man who murdered Ruth Hill. He won't get away. That's a promise."

"Even if it's a cop?"

Dane's eyes flashed silent trouble. "You know the answer to that," he said, giving in and digging for another cigarette from the pack. "I work the cases Commander Hoenig assigns me. I work them all the same. I play no favorites, never will."

Jake wanted to believe him, but something Bruce Drummond had said about Boston's involvement in a Cambridge murder case made it difficult. "All cases aren't the same, Tommy. Some have strings attached. Who's pulling them on this one?"

"Drop it, Jake," Dane said, lighting up. "Drop it."

"Watch that you don't get wrapped up in those strings, Tommy. Even good cops like you can get tangled."

Dane pulled in a lung full of smoke. He blew it out and changed the subject. "We really ought to get together, Jake. Once this is over, what do you say? I miss the old times."

"You know where to reach me," Jake said, taking one last look around and adding Dane to the list of friends not telling him the complete truth.

Number 28 Commonwealth Avenue was an enormous and elaborate Victorian mansion that fell victim to greedy developers in the 1980s. Back then, any building not falling in on itself was divided into condominiums and sold to yuppies who swarmed into Boston for a few years of raising hell before settling down in the suburbs. Now the trend was showing signs of reversal. A few of the finer old buildings were being returned to their original splendor. Twenty-eight Commonwealth Avenue was the address where Gloria Gorham had plunked down her million. The architect estimated that another $500,000 would be needed to restore the place to a single-family home. They were numbers that Jake shrank from and numbers that Gloria, with her family wealth, considered the basic cost of doing business on one of Boston's most famous streets.

Jake pulled around into the alley and parked next to the dumpster, which took up both of the deeded parking spaces that came with the town house. Plaster dust from the debris rose in puffs as parts of broken walls from the fourth floor rumbled through the chute and crashed into the metal container.

Jake found Gloria on the first floor. She was dressed in working jeans and a large dark green cotton sweater that emphasized her large green eyes. Her light brown hair was held behind her ears with a gold filigree clasp that matched her earrings.

Jake stepped behind her as Watson sniffed in the direction of a worker's closed lunch pail. Jake put his arms around Gloria and kissed her lightly on the neck. She leaned against him, letting him hold her weight.

"Wonderful, isn't it?" Her voice was full of the possible, her gaze on what Jake saw as a wrecked living room.

"You're wonderful," he said, taking the easy route. "What are the contractors going to save?" he asked.

Gloria stepped out of his grasp. "The parquet floors, the dentil moldings, the marble fireplaces, some of the trim. Everything they can that's original. Do you remember the bath on the second floor? The one with the old claw-footed tub? I want them to keep that. It has great charm, don't you think?" she asked, bending down to Watson, who'd come over for a hug of his own.

Jake liked the look of the six-over-six windows. The view they offered was of the Commonwealth Avenue esplanade, famous for its mature trees, gardens, and bronze statues. He could imagine quiet, snowy nights together with Gloria, admiring the view. Loud banging on the floors above brought him back to the present.

"While you were spending a fortune this morning, a case dropped in my lap," Jake said.

"Another one?" Gloria gave Watson one last scratch, then stood. "Anything I'd be interested in?"

"Afraid so. A woman was raped and strangled on Cambridge Common while we were away sailing."

Gloria's eyes compressed. "That's horrible," she said emphatically. "Every woman's nightmare is a death like that. And on the Common?"

Jake nodded.

"You're not safe anywhere nowadays," Gloria said, emitting a small sigh. "Are there suspects?"

"So I'm led to believe," Jake said, explaining his conversation with Lieutenant Dane. Jake left out his suspicion that a cop might be involved. "Tommy says the victim had been around."

"Justifying her murder?" Gloria shot back.

"I didn't say that."

"No, but that's what a remark like that means. It's demeaning, Jake: 'A woman who's been around gets what she deserves.' Even a hooker shouldn't die strangled to death at night in a deserted park."

"I didn't say she was a hooker," Jake said defensively.

"Then what was she?"

"A secretary at Harvard University by the name of Ruth Hill."

A loud boom from above shook the ceiling, rattling the crystal chandelier that hung in the center of the room. Gloria looked up like Chicken Little expecting the sky to fall.

She cut Jake a pleading glance. "I'd better see what's going on. This is my baby. I want it to be perfect."

"Understood."

She gave Jake a quick, apologetic kiss. "I didn't mean to snap at you, Jake. It's just that the poor woman died a horrifying death. There's no reason for Dane or anyone else to hurt her any more. Her reputation may be all her family has left." She gave Jake a warm smile. "I'm proud of you for looking into it, Jake. Ruth Hill's very lucky you're on her side," Gloria said, then raced up the stairs toward more ominous sounds.

Jake watched her go, then turned to Watson. "Hear that, Watson? We're on Ruth Hill's side."

Watson loved being spoken to and wagged his tail in appreciation.

"Let's go see what we can do for her."

Watson barked a response, then followed Jake to the door.

Chapter 4

Back in the alley and in his Saab, Jake picked up the cellular phone and called the number Drummond had given him for Ruth Hill's office. After a few rings, a man's winsome voice answered.

"Psychology Department," the man said. "Professor Zimmer here."

Jake introduced himself, then asked if he could speak with someone who knew Ruth Hill regarding the circumstances of her death.

"Are you being purposefully dense?" Zimmer asked harshly. "The 'circumstances,' as you call it, are that Miss Hill's murder is one more example of society's decay. I've written about it for years. The world we're living in is crumbling around us. It's falling apart right before our very eyes. It's disgusting. There's no other way to describe it. It is *disgusting!*"

He's given this lecture before, Jake thought and cradled the phone against his ear with his shoulder. "I'm sure you're right, professor, but I was wondering—"

"It's terribly disruptive to the university," Zimmer cut in. "And to our department. Vicki Shaw has taken it worst of all. She can't teach any of her classes, she is so distraught."

Drummond had mentioned a Vicki Shaw. "Would she be the same person who—"

"To whom Ruth was assigned," the professor interrupted again. "That is correct," Zimmer said as if it pained him to explain. "The Psych Department provides limited secretarial support to graduate students nearing completion of their dissertations. Ruth was work-ing with Vicki in that capacity."

"Doing what?" Jake asked.

"Word processing, organizing the bibliography, things like that."

"Any research help?" Jake asked, recalling that Drummond said Ruth went to the *Herald* office to look up something in the files.

"Research?" The word sounded bitter in Zimmer's mouth. "You can't know much about Harvard if you think a secretary would ever be permitted to conduct research for one of our graduate students. Besides, Vicki's dissertation was in its final stages. All her research was completed. That's the main reason Ruth was assigned to her. All that was left was a polish edit and the final typing."

"Then Ruth Hill worked with no one else?"

"That's right. Until that dissertation was finished, Ruth had no other assignments. And that in itself is curious," Zimmer added. "Ruth had a reputation for being quick and accurate. That's the rea-son she was hired. But that quickness wasn't the case with Vicki's manuscript. It had slowed to a stop."

"Any reason you can pinpoint?" Jake asked, taking the phone back in his hand.

"None." The admission seemed deflating. "Not that I'm directly involved, mind you, but word does get around. I've been worried about Vicki finishing, quite honestly." Zimmer sounded genuine in his concern.

"And, you think—"

"I don't know how to view it," Zimmer said, cutting off Jake yet again. "It might be that Vicki is rethinking part of her work, or it might be—or might have been, I should say—Ruth's problem. I don't believe that Ruth had been here long enough to complete her final performance appraisal. She was just recently employed, you un-derstand."

"How long ago?" Jake asked, finally getting in a completed ques-tion.

"Three months, maybe. To be sure, I'd have to have the depart-ment secretary check the records," Zimmer said. Then added, "Maybe Ruth wasn't as competent as we were led to believe. We'll never know, will we? All I know for certain is that Vicki's dissertation work wasn't going as fast as it should have. Who's to blame, I don't know. I do know that Vicki's research is important and should be completed for all to see. It simply must be," the professor said, an urgency in his voice.

Jake asked what Vicki Shaw was studying.

"The behavioral patterns of women serial killers. It's a fascinating study," Zimmer said. "I hope she pulls herself together after this terrible Ruth Hill business and gets it finished. I'm afraid it won't be soon, however. As I said, Vicki is taking this very hard."

"I can imagine," Jake said. "I'd like to speak with her."

Zimmer gruffed into the phone. "You'll have to find her first," he said. "Lieutenant Dane is one step ahead of you there."

"You've spoken with Tommy?" Jake asked, not surprised.

"Yes. Right after Ruth's body was found. He was most persistent," Zimmer said, his voice indicating he didn't like being cornered. "He made me feel like a suspect. I'm not, of course, but policemen like to make you feel that way. One of their mind games, no doubt. I was surprised it worked on me, being in the field of psychology as I am. Still, I didn't like it."

You're not supposed to, Jake thought. He asked if the professor knew where Vicki Shaw might be.

"No idea," Zimmer said. "But if I'm any judge of character, Lieutenant Dane might know by now. He struck me as being tenacious. Why don't you confer with him for answers to your questions?"

Love to, Jake thought, only Tommy's not answering.

"Anything else?" Zimmer asked, making it clear he had little else to add.

"Not now," Jake said. He thanked the professor for his time and hung up just as another ton of rubble slammed into the dumpster. Watson nosed the car window, watching the plaster dust settle over the Saab. He cocked his head toward Jake, who said, "Think we ought to try to confer with Tommy Dane?"

Watson cranked his head farther to the right, as if such a move would make the words understandable. He held the pose, his eyes questioning his master.

Jake patted him, saying, "Confer. It's a Harvard word." He tapped Dane's number into the cellular phone and waited.

"Homicide. Detective Morgan speaking."

Jake glanced at the phone as if it had betrayed him. "I thought this was Tommy Dane's number," he said.

"Used to be. The lieutenant's been temporarily reassigned."

"To what?"

Morgan asked who was asking.

"Come on, Morgan. People say my crusty voice is unmistakable. Use your imagination. It's Jake. Jake Eaton calling from afar."

"Not far enough, to hear Lieutenant Dane tell it," Morgan said, as if he were one step ahead of the private detective and enjoying it.

"Where is Tommy?" Jake asked.

"Playing in the big time. The lieutenant's head of a special task force, Jake. He's got a new office and a handful of Internal Affairs men to boss around."

"What's this all about, Morgan?" Jake asked. "What the hell's going on over there?"

"That's all I can say, Jake. Except to pass along a message the lieutenant left for you." Jake could almost see Morgan smiling as he continued. "Lieutenant Dane said when you came poking around to tell you that he knows who you're working for."

It was Jake's time to cut someone off. "I never told him," Jake snapped. "How did he find out?"

"He waved the magic wand," Morgan said slyly. "Guess who popped out of the hat?"

Jake wasn't keen on Morgan's humor. "If you've got something to say, say it."

"In due time," Morgan said, enjoying himself. "Out of this hat pops the old reporter himself. Not a rabbit at all."

"Impossible," Jake said. Drummond would never tip his hand to the police.

"Not impossible," Morgan said sharply. "He stood in Lieutenant Dane's office and announced that you were looking into Ruth Hill's murder. Your client has a big mouth, Jake. He spilled the beans, and we weren't even beating him with a rubber hose."

"Very funny."

"That's the point, Jake. There's nothing funny about any of this. It's serious stuff," Morgan said, meaning it. "Dane wants you to get that through your thick skull. He said to tell you that Bruce Drummond was not going to use this murder investigation to sell papers."

"That's not my style," Jake said. "I wasn't hired to increase anyone's circulation."

"Believe what you want," Morgan responded. "The bottom line, Jake: Tell Drummond to back off."

"Is that a threat, Morgan?" Jake asked.

"No. No, threat. It's a message from a friend of yours, Tommy Dane. Any reply?"

"Yeah," Jake said. "Tell Tommy I'm a lot of things, but a marionette isn't one of them."

"What's that supposed to mean?"

"It means to watch out for the strings, Morgan. Tommy will understand," Jake said irritably.

Jake put down the phone. The idea that Drummond had more to explain drifted through his mind like black ink.

Chapter 5

Jacob Wirth's is a steamy German restaurant in Boston's theater district not far from the New England Medical Center and Chinatown. It has an Old World feel to it, a little piece of nineteenth-century Bavaria plopped down on a busy Boston street.

Bruce Drummond used Jacob Wirth's—and dozens of other eateries around the city—as a second office where he could mix the newspaper business with pleasure in whatever proportions he wanted. He was seated in the booth farthest back and waved when Jake came in.

"Drink?" Drummond asked as Jake slid in the opposite seat.

"Sam Adams."

"A 'Sam' it is," Drummond said, holding up an empty bottle and two fingers to the passing waitress. "I've got a staff meeting in an hour."

"This won't take long," Jake said, his tone serious. "If you thought I was half asleep when you hired me this morning, think again, Bruce."

Drummond's expression soured. "What's this all about?" he asked warily.

"Confidentiality. It's just as important in my line of work as it is in yours." Jake's expression hardened. "Why did you tell Tommy Dane I was working for you?"

"Who said I did?" Drummond asked, sensing immediately that Jake was in no mood for a Socratic dialogue. "All right, I know I shouldn't have, but—"

"You shouldn't even have talked to Dane. That became my job once I took your case. What burns me, Drummond, is that you know all that. Still, you bungle into—"

Drummond rose to the challenge. "I wouldn't call it bungling," he said.

"What the hell would you call it?"

"Applying pressure," Drummond offered as the waitress returned and began to pour.

Jake glared at Drummond until the waitress had gone. "Pressure on whom? Not Dane. He'd flick you away like a fly."

"Already has several times. Trouble is," Drummond admitted with a smirk, "I keep coming back."

"Looking for what?" Jake asked irritably. "Come on, Drum. I know there's more to this than the murder of Ruth Hill. A hell of a lot more, and I'm here for answers." Jake sipped his beer and waited.

Drummond leaned forward, his voice low. "All right, but you won't like it."

Jake said nothing, his face like a stone statue.

"Rumors started weeks ago," Drummond began. "An in-house inquiry was coming down so hot that Internal Affairs wanted nothing to do with it. A special task force was set up to do the dirty work. Lieutenant Dane was pulled from Homicide Division and put in charge."

"What made the work dirty?" Jake asked.

"The murder of Lori Churchwell," Drummond answered gravely. "The way she was found naked on a bed with a red bow tied around her neck brought back chilling memories of the Boston Strangler."

"That's old news, Drum," Jake reminded him. "The Boston Strangler went to prison more than thirty years ago."

Drummond raised his hands in submission. "Hey, you came for information. You don't want to hear any, fine with me."

Jake backed off and took a sip of beer.

"I've been knocking around this town a long time," Drummond said. "I'm not the only one who thought the original Strangler investigation was as rotten as fish heads."

"That case has been analyzed to death, Drum. No official wrongdoing was ever uncovered."

"Correct," Drummond said unhappily. "Which is why it's curious as hell that some official higher-ups decided to look into the Strangler case again right after Lori Churchwell's body turned up."

Jake asked about the higher-ups and listened as Drummond spit out the names of Commander Ronald Hoenig and Senator Conrad Fowler. In the original case, then Lieutenant Hoenig was put in charge because of his reputation as a tireless investigator; Fowler was the newly elected attorney general for the state of Massachusetts. Hoenig and Fowler were the heart and soul of the Strangler investigation. Both men have gone on to respected and successful careers.

"Trouble was," Drummond continued, "before Tommy Dane could look into much, a second victim turned up."

Jake felt a prickle along his shoulders. "You mean that victim number two wasn't Ruth Hill?" he asked.

Drummond nodded stiffly. "That's right. The second was Sylvia Reardon. Ruth Hill was number three. All three were raped and strangled." Drummond drank half his beer in one gulp, then swiped the corners of his mouth with a napkin. "I told you before, Ruth Hill's death was only a small part of something that began years back."

"You're reaching, Drum," Jake said. "I don't know all the facts, but you're reaching."

Drummond smiled knowingly. "Am I?" He let the question hang, then answered it himself. "Maybe in the past I believed in what wasn't there, but not this time, Jake. This time, I'm right. This time, I'm on the verge of proving it."

As Jake knew, "it" was the truth behind the Boston Strangler case. It was Drummond's passion, the quest that gave his life meaning and drove those around him—Jake included—to distraction.

Jake was just a child in 1962 when the Boston Strangler first struck. Drummond was new on his job as a beat crime reporter for the old *Record American*. Two years later, after thirteen women had died horrible deaths, Albert Henry DeSalvo was arrested as the Boston Strangler.

"I must have written a thousand column inches about that story," Drummond lamented. "I could have written ten thousand, but all the news outlets were giving Boston PD a break. Cops were sick of all the killings, the city was tired of being afraid. The press got lazy and let the cops running the Strangler investigation dictate what the truth was. I guess you could say we were all bone tired of those murders. When you're tired, you make mistakes. Mine was in not paying attention to my instincts."

"And what did they tell you?"

"That Albert DeSalvo was not the Boston Strangler."

Jake felt surrounded by an uneasiness brought on by the possibility that Drummond's suspicions were right. You couldn't live in Boston and not know the theories regarding Albert DeSalvo's possible innocence and of a police cover-up. Over the years, Jake had listened suspiciously to them all, dismissing most as local versions of conspiracy theories that often surround dramatic cases, such as John Kennedy's death in Dallas. Were there two assassins? Another shooter on the grassy knoll? A lot of questions were asked in a way that made the answers fit the theory. An equal number had been asked about DeSalvo's guilt, but the facts remained: Albert Henry DeSalvo went to prison for those thirteen murders, and the men in charge of the investigation—then Attorney General Conrad Fowler and then Lieutenant Ronald Hoenig—were investigated, but they were never charged with any wrongdoing.

Still, Drummond persisted. "You know me, Jake. I've thought for years that DeSalvo might have been an easy patsy to close a hot-potato case."

"You and a dozen others," Jake reminded him.

"Hey, I'm not suggesting anything original. But there is one big difference," Drummond said with pride. "I've stuck with it; the others didn't. I've kept digging. The murders of Churchwell, Reardon, and Ruth Hill have convinced me I'm right."

"It took three women to convince you?" Jake chided. "Why didn't you come to me sooner?"

Drummond's expression saddened. "Because I thought I could deal with it on my own. I thought—"

"You could run in, camera flashing, headlines splashed all over the front page so you could sell a few thousand more papers."

Drummond eyes locked on Jake. "Who gave you a crazy idea like that?"

"Dane."

"And you believe him?" he asked as if he'd been hit by a low blow.

"I'm here to find out if I should."

"Not a ringing vote of confidence for me, is it, Jake?" Drummond said bluntly. "A cop—the master of misinformation when misinformation is required to take your mind off the real issue—drops a hint of doubt on you regarding my motive, and you buy into it." Drummond shook his head in disbelief. "Look what Dane's doing, Jake. He's making me the bad guy. He's taking the focus off Boston PD and the murder of three women and putting it on me."

"Then you're not running these stories?" Jake pressed.

"Correct," Drummond said bitterly. "At least, not now. And certainly not in my paper. Dane knows that's impossible."

"Why impossible?"

"Because Boston PD has put a lid on the facts surrounding those three murders. Everything is 'under investigation.' 'No comment' is the answer given when any reporter asks for details. There's nothing to put in the paper, Jake, or believe me, I'd have it in," Drummond said, his frustration apparent as he slid from the booth. He stood straight, pressing the wrinkles out of his suit coat with the flat of his hand. "I told you that you wouldn't like it, Jake, but the man scheming you is Tommy Dane, not me."

Or both, Jake thought, saying nothing.

"I guess the only question left is, are you on my side or not?" Drummond asked. "If you're not, I'm going to find the answers I need without you."

"You're still my client, Drum, if that's what you're asking," Jake said, not picking sides.

"That's all I wanted to hear," Drummond said, taking a personal check from his pocket. He put it on the table. "The first week in advance," he said, then left.

Jake glanced at the check. He put it away, thinking that it wasn't enough if Ruth Hill's murder led a path to dirty cops and Tommy Dane.

No amount was.

Chapter 6

The dust and gravel had barely settled when the car jolted to a stop and a big man got out. He walked up the path to a small shed. As he opened the door, the air filled with the stench of soiled cages and the grating, unpleasant sound of barking dogs.

He had never been in prison, but he knew what it felt like. His freedom had been ripped away with pills, mood levelers the doctor called them. Downers. Something to take the edge off, something to make him more manageable for his sister Sarah.

A saint the family called her, but none too loudly. A wealthy recluse was the public front. No, Sarah hadn't wanted to marry. No, she enjoyed the simple life on the family estate with her ample library, her music, her charities, her close friends.

The truth was, she had little choice about the direction of her life unless she wanted to see the family name ruined as her brother marched off to prison a convicted mass murderer. Why suffer the indignity when she could keep him isolated, drugged, and cared for? The family would see to the details. All she had to do was be there, and she had been—most of the time—until she died.

Poor Sarah.

The big man shook the thought. No, not poor Sarah. She was more warden than sister. She deserved to die. When he stopped taking those pills, he saw it clearly. Not only did she deserve it, she wanted to die. He obliged.

He moved past the pens, inspecting the different breeds, detached from their eager, friendly faces. He wanted neither. He was looking for something far from friendly.

Head bent against the dismal wind, the owner of the pet shelter opened the shed door. One of those bells shopkeepers use to alert themselves of customers rang. The big man hadn't noticed when he'd entered. He'd barely noticed it now over the chorus of baying dogs.

The owner, a thin, frail man in his fifties, instantly felt wary of the person before him. "You the man called about the guard dog?" he asked, eyeing the size of his customer.

"Two."

"That's right. Two dogs, for a . . . ?"

The big man looked back at the pens. "I didn't say."

The owner nodded reluctantly. "Don't have to, of course. It helps me give you direction is all. Advice, you understand. A lot depends on the size of the place to be guarded—whether it's inside or out. A bunch of things to take into consideration when picking the right dog."

"Let's have a look," the big man said, leading the way.

Jake parked in the Commercial Wharf parking lot and let Watson out to run while he unlocked the marina gate. Below, on the docks, two men were covering a cabin cruiser with blue plastic to protect it from the burgeoning Boston winter.

Jake waited for Watson to dart in, closed the gate, and walked down the ramp made steeper by the unusually low tide. On the dock, Watson slammed his paws down playfully. His eyes rolled up, exposing white crescents as he spun chasing his tail. For a reason Jake never understood, Watson turned into a ball of spirited mischief once on the floating dock inside the marina. In a way, it was how Jake himself felt when he approached *Gamecock,* Gloria's pre–World War II wooden sloop. It wasn't the sloop that interested him as much as its lovely owner.

He and Gloria had been together for more than three years, evidence that opposites attract. Gloria was a well-bred, aristocratic Yankee and a natural beauty. Jake was as roughhouse as his canine partner, red-blooded—not blue—and more physically fit than handsome.

They both enjoyed a sailing weekend to Martha's Vineyard or Nantucket. Gloria had grown up with the sport; Jake had to be taught. Fortunately, Gloria was a patient teacher. Maybe that was his attraction to her. Jake was a self-taught adventurer, willing to bite into life at any point. Gloria had been fed life in the finely measured portions of finishing schools. She had sampled much but had experienced little to the fullest. With Jake, she could keep what was familiar and comfortable but also explore new realms. She grew to love Jake for his willingness to try whatever she asked. Even the symphony, sans tie.

Watson collapsed on his forepaws, barking without menace as Jake boarded the boat. The racket brought Gloria up from below. She was carrying cheese and crackers on a wooden tray. Her bright eyes went from Jake to the grinning dog, who raised his head, waiting for an invitation.

"Well, come on," Gloria encouraged, watching Watson leap aboard in one swift motion. She put down the tray and scruffed his hairy neck. "How's the best dog in the world?" she purred, sending Watson twisting onto his back, thrusting powerful legs skyward.

"I think that means he's damn fine," Jake said, helping Gloria stand. He kissed her, adding, "I'm not so bad myself—now."

Gloria stepped back, her head tilted, a coy smile on her lips. "That makes two of us," she said, heading back down the companionway steps and into the galley. In seconds, she was back carrying Jake's preferred cocktail, a vodka gimlet on the rocks.

She'd made two, hers with more lime.

Jake sipped the drink, savoring the slow burn as it trickled down his throat. "First-rate," he said, raising his glass.

Gloria returned the gesture. "Today, at the house, I was thinking how nice it will be to come down to the boat only when I want to."

"Tired of living aboard?" Jake asked, wondering how she'd managed to stay aboard during the past year. Of course, he knew the answer: she wanted to.

Gloria shrugged. "Not tired of it, no. *Gamecock*'s too much a part of me ever to be tired of her. But I think a little distance will do us both good."

"Absence makes the heart grow fonder?" Jake quipped.

"Something like that," she said, seeing the sport in Jake's eyes. "What's the matter? You don't think clichés are true?"

"Maybe."

"I had a Harvard professor in one of my literature classes explain that clichés are overused precisely because they are often based on truth."

Jake grew instantly more attentive, reminded that Gloria had flown through Harvard, getting her BA in three years, her MBA in one.

"Your old university came up in conversation today," he said.

"Oh?"

"Yeah, in a roundabout sort of way."

"Not surprising. We Harvard types are everywhere."

Including the morgue, Jake thought but didn't say it. "Ruth Hill was a Harvard grad."

The smile dropped from Gloria's lips. "Oh," she said, this time softly. "I forget the sort of conversations you sometimes have looking into people's deaths. You think there's a connection between her murder and Harvard?"

"Not ruling anything out," Jake answered. "All I know for sure is that Ruth Hill was typing the final draft of a graduate student's dissertation concerning women serial killers."

"Right up Neil's alley," Gloria remarked, returning Jake's quizzical glance. "Neil Ebberhardt. You remember. Three weeks ago with all the cameras flashing?"

"Ah, the Ebberhardt Institute," Jake said, referring to one of Harvard's more famous research facilities. "How could I forget?" Jake teased. "But I have. Refresh my memory."

"Come on, Jake," Gloria said. "Unless you were lying, you said you had a good time. Except for the reception afterward and that nuisance photographer."

"Oh, that. Opening night at the symphony," he said, replaying the party scene backstage with the champagne, canapés, mink coats, and black ties.

Gloria saw Jake's familiar look of drifting off. "I introduced you to Neil Ebberhardt, remember?"

"Not really," Jake admitted. "But I do remember the Haydn Cello

Concerto in D. It was lovely. I did my best to tune out the party. A little on the boring side for my tastes. Which one of the gray hairs in black tails was Neil?"

Gloria feigned offense. "You're incorrigible, do you know that?"

"One of my strengths."

"And stubborn."

Jake tossed Watson a cracker. "Very," he admitted. "Now, what about Neil?"

"Early retirement. Does that ring a bell?"

"A bell is ringing," Jake said, remembering what Gloria had told him. At a board meeting for the symphony's Youth Concert Series, Ebberhardt announced he was stepping down from the institute he had founded more than thirty years before.

Neil had been a young man then, the type of student for which Harvard is famous: bright, talented, wealthy, and driven to succeed. And succeed Ebberhardt had, by taking scattered disciplines, adding computer technology and enormous databases, and refining the procedures for identifying serial killers by use of their psychological profile. Police departments all over the world were quickly knocking at Neil Ebberhardt's door, a door that soon opened into the institute that carries his name. Once the FBI adopted Ebberhardt's method, Neil was assured of his place in the annals of criminology.

"How old is Ebberhardt?" Jake asked.

Gloria shrugged. "Late fifties, I'd guess. For years, he was touted as the youngest institute director Harvard had ever hired."

"Sounds like a classic whiz kid," Jake said.

"He was," Gloria agreed. "Of course, circumstances played a part. If Boston hadn't been in a panic, Neil might never have tested his theory so soon. I've heard him talk about it often. He's always said he wasn't comfortable tackling a major crime first thing, but that's what the Strangler case was."

Jake pursed his lips as the conversation came back to him. Neil Ebberhardt had made his reputation creating the behavioral profile that led to the arrest of Albert DeSalvo.

"I don't remember much about that time, do you?" Jake asked, tossing Watson another cracker.

Gloria shrugged. "Not much, but what I do remember is vivid because of my mother. I was just a small child, but I can recall a sense of being afraid in my own house. I know that my mother did her best to hide it from me, but she was frightened knowing that a man was out there killing women. Everybody wondered who was going to be next." She stirred her cocktail, looking inquisitively at Jake. "Why do you ask?"

"Just curious."

"You always are, Jake, but you don't ask about things that aren't relevant," Gloria told him. "What's so important about the Boston Strangler after all these years?"

"The honest answer is, I don't know," he said, then he summarized Bruce Drummond's speculation that the Strangler had returned. "If Drummond is correct, Ruth Hill's death might be the latest in a long line of Strangler victims."

Gloria furrowed her brow, surprised but reluctant to believe what she'd just heard. "Ruth Hill?" she asked. "What on earth could connect her to a case that was solved about the time she was born?"

"Good question."

"And a good answer?"

Jake thought a moment, ignoring Watson's begging stare. "I don't know, but research is a pretty good guess," he said.

"I thought she was typing a dissertation."

"She was." Jake spoke as he thought it through. "It's interesting that Neil Ebberhardt and Vicki Shaw both had an interest in serial killers."

"Who's Vicki Shaw?" Gloria asked, giving in to Watson. She took a cracker from the tray and set it on her knee. Watson snapped it up.

"Vicki Shaw is the Harvard grad student Ruth Hill was working with."

"Have you spoken to her?" Gloria asked.

"Can't," Jake said. "She disappeared right after Ruth Hill was murdered."

"Disappeared?" Gloria repeated, trying to connect something that wouldn't connect. "How do you mean 'disappeared'?"

Jake recounted his phone call with Professor Zimmer, then said, "Zimmer didn't seem too concerned that Vicki wasn't teaching her classes."

"So?"

Jake shrugged. "So my guess is Vicki called in from wherever she is and said she needed a few days to regroup. People do that, you know."

"Does that mean you're going to wait until she turns up?"

Jake took another sip of his drink. "It means I'm going to look for her," he said.

"Now?" Gloria asked, sliding closer.

Jake looked down into her delightfully inviting eyes. "It crossed my mind," he said with little conviction. "It could be changed."

"Let's try," Gloria said, draping her arms around Jake's neck.

He put his mouth next to hers. "We're out here for all to see."

"Makes them envious."

"I'm a little envious myself," Jake whispered. "Damn lucky we found each other."

"Agreed."

Jake pulled her closer, the lobe of her ear in his lips, his open hands stroking the length of her back. *Gamecock* seemed to rock them closer together, and in seconds they were below.

Chapter 7

Jake knew Vicki Shaw's neighborhood well. Long before he met Gloria, he dated a woman from that part of Cambridge who lived for Indian food, black-and-white films, and noisy bedroom romps, in that order. Spicy curry dinners often began a few blocks from Vicki's address near Cambridge's Central Square, an eclectic mix of classes, culture, and cuisine, one subway stop inbound from Harvard.

Jake turned the Saab onto Prospect Street, took the second left, then pulled to a stop under a big oak in front of a rehabbed 1920s triple-decker. Someone had taken great pains on a fancy paint job that contrasted dark green clapboards with wine-colored shutters and trim. Glad someone else did it, Jake thought. He prized the simple life of a condo. He cracked open the driver's side window for Watson and got out.

Eagerly, he climbed the porch steps. The brass plate over the buzzer indicated that Vicki Shaw and Jan Rybicki lived on the third floor. Jake pressed the intercom button, waited, then rang it again. In a few minutes, the off-putting tone known well to unwanted salesmen came through the small speaker.

"Yes? Who is it?"

Jake introduced himself as a private detective looking into some trouble at Harvard. "Vicki Shaw?" he asked hopefully.

"Vicki's not here. What do you want?" the female voice questioned.

"I'd like to start by coming in." Jake waited for the buzzer to sound and the lock to release. When it didn't, he said, "It will only take a few minutes." He glanced again at the name plate. "Miss Rybicki, is it? Five minutes max. Please."

"You can have five. But *only* five. I'm expecting company," the voice said, the door buzzing open.

Jake entered and climbed the wooden steps toward the slightly built woman in her late twenties waiting at the top. Even though it was just before noon, she wore an elegant black silk blouse with padded shoulders over a pair of black-and-white-checked slacks with cuffs that broke just above her spiked heels. She fit right into the trendy night crowd, Jake thought and extended his hand.

"Jan Rybicki?" he asked.

Her handshake was firm, sending the message of equality. "That's me," she said, and asked for ID.

Jake presented his detective's license, which she scrutinized intently until she finally stepped back, letting Jake enter. The floor-through apartment was dominated by an enormous rolltop walnut desk at the far end of the living room. Jake stepped toward it. Loose papers and books occupied every level surface. A ceiling fan circulated the heated air around the spacious room.

"Vicki's not as neat as I am," Jan said, motioning Jake toward an old, overstuffed chair. "My room is through there." She pointed down a long, narrow hall. "This is where Vicki works when she's home. She hasn't been home lately."

Jake got right to the point. "Do you know where she is?" he asked.

"Not really."

"Meaning?"

"Meaning I've spoken to her," Jan said. "She didn't say where she was staying, but she wanted me to know she was all right in case her family called."

Jake asked about her family and learned they were all in California. Jake sat, his attention back on the papers on Vicki's desk. "Is that part of her dissertation?"

"I suppose," Jan answered. "We didn't talk much about it, if you want the truth. It was one of the ground rules for being roommates.

She wouldn't try to psychoanalyze me, and I wouldn't try to get her to drop everything and become a flight attendant." Jan spun in place with the movements of a runway model showing off her outfit. "You like? I couldn't wait to try it on. Guess where I got it? London. London's hot right now. Fashion, restaurants, clubs, you name it." She sat in the wicker love seat, beaming.

"When was the last time you saw Vicki?" Jake asked, a little nonplussed by her performance but struck by her vitality and charm.

Jan rolled her eyes. "Let's see, the police asked all that. I want to be consistent, you know. It was Wednesday, last week. I was off on a Paris run. I had some time coming and took it in London. Scott's a pilot. He's who I'm expecting. We go all over together but seldom here. That's another rule Vicki and I have. No friends can spend the night. Taboo! I've lost more roommates that way. It starts out as a weekend sort of thing, then he's around all the time. It's trouble, you know? I mean, I may not even like the guy, still he's living here. No way."

"Did Vicki have a boyfriend who caused you some trouble?" Jake asked.

Jan shook her head. "I never saw her have a date. Which is not to say she shared Ruth Hill's social interests, if you know what I mean."

"I've heard," Jake said. "Ruth's fascination with men may have been a factor in her death."

"What?" Jan gasped. "Whose fascination with men? Ruth Hill was gay."

Jake felt his face flush. Dane had set him up with a lie, and Jan Rybicki had knocked him over with the truth. "I heard otherwise," Jake admitted.

"Then you heard wrong," Jan said in a firm, precise voice. "Does it bother you? I know some men who can't imagine women sleeping together."

"Not at all," Jake said honestly. "It's just that I heard something different about Ruth's preference. I must've been mistaken," he said. He asked about Vicki's friends.

"I can't say she has many," Jan said. "It's like I told the police, Vicki is pretty quiet. No social life to speak of. She spends her time working on whatever she's working on over at Harvard. I don't know too much about it, really. It don't interest me."

"How much *do* you know?"

Jan rolled her shoulders forward in a small arc. "Well," she said as if about to reveal something top secret. "I know that Vicki almost gave up a time or two. She was hitting a brick wall over at that institute."

"The Ebberhardt?" Jake prompted.

"That sounds right." Jan shifted in her seat, then brushed back her short brown hair with the fingers of one hand. "Vicki said graduate students are sometimes treated like trash. I told her she should be a flight attendant for one day."

"I'm sure you can take care of yourself," Jake told her, hoping someday to meet Vicki Shaw so he could draw his own conclusion. "Did Vicki tell you what her troubles were at the institute?"

"No, only that she wasn't welcome there. But it's a glorified library, right? How can they keep you out?" Jan asked incredulously. "I'd have raised hell, but Vicki isn't the type. She's more calculating, you know? She picks her spots, then makes her move. She's no dummy, let me tell you. Neither was Ruth. They made a good team."

"Then you saw them working together?" Jake asked.

"Sure. Lots of times." She gestured toward the desk. "They would spend hours going over this and that, getting more and more paranoid that someone might find out what they were doing. Me, I'd go batty pouring over all those pages. I don't know how the three of them did it."

"Three?" Jake repeated. "Who was the third?"

"The newspaperman," Jan answered, scrunching wrinkles into her forehead as she sifted around in her memory for an answer. "Oh, what is his name?" she mumbled.

Jake closed his eyes, but the image of his client wouldn't go away. "Bruce Drummond," he finally said.

Jan brightened. "That's the one. He's sort of cute, you know? Old enough to be my father, but . . ."

But what, Jake didn't care. His disappointment in Drummond's failure to tell him the truth about his relationship with Vicki and Ruth Hill showed in his eyes.

Jan saw the look. "What?" she asked. "Did I say something?"

Jake shook himself out of his lethargy. "No," he said, then asked what Drummond's connection was to Vicki.

"The book, I guess," Jan answered as the intercom buzzer sounded. "That's all the three of them have been working on for the past several weeks," she said, heading for the intercom as if pulled by a magnet.

Jake got to his feet. "You mean the dissertation?" he said.

"I don't think so," Jan said, clearly distracted. "Like I said, I don't know a lot about Vicki's comings and goings. I'm just not here enough." Jan quickly pressed the door release without asking who was there.

Jake brought that to her attention. "Bad habit," he said. "I'd be more careful until Vicki turns up. No telling what might crawl up the stairs."

"It's Scott," she said, dismissing Jake's concern. "Besides, your five minutes are up."

When Jan, grinning in anticipation, stepped into the hall to greet her guest, Jake went to Vicki's paper-strewn desk. Trying to make sense of the clutter, he began examining a stack of printed text when Jan popped back inside.

"Go ahead and look if you want," she said. "The police did."

Lieutenant Dane?" Jake asked.

"Sounds familiar. Is he the little wiry one?" Jan tossed out.

"That's him."

"Yes, well, like I told him: look but don't touch. Vicki is very picky about stuff on her desk. When she comes back, I don't want her raising hell with me because it's all messed up," Jan said, then went back into the hall.

"Thanks," Jake said, knowing his time to look was running out as he heard the footsteps on the stairs grow louder.

He scanned the desk. Toward the front were stacks of loose pages written in dry, academic language. A paper pile entitled *Wake the Bear* caught his eye. It didn't sound like any dissertation title he'd ever heard of. He turned the page and he started to read when a man's voice greeted Jan. Jake folded the page inside his coat pocket just as the lusty couple came into the room.

From the same pocket, Jake removed a business card. He held it
out. Jan took it, making brief introductions. "Scotty and I—"
   "Of course." Jake went to the door. "If you think of anything . . ."
   "I will. I'll call. Promise," Jan said, as if she'd said the same to others and didn't mean it then either.

Chapter 8

Jake left Jan Rybicki and drove down Western Avenue, his jaw tight with frustration. Working with a client who never told all of the truth was the part of the job that Jake hated. He hated it more when the client was also a friend. But even without Drummond's help, some things were coming together.

One was the explanation as to why Vicki's dissertation wasn't finished: she wasn't working on it. She and Ruth—if Jan with her sketchy information could be believed—were working on a book with Drummond. Is that why Drum wasn't chafing at the bit to fill the pages of the *Herald* with stories about the Strangler? Was he saving it all for a book? But writing with a partner? Jake wondered. Drummond was such a loner. Even if he wanted to, could he work with anyone? Or, he thought, maybe Vicki was more source than writing partner. Jake decided to find out.

He picked up the cellular phone and called The *Herald*. The receptionist told him that Bruce Drummond wasn't in. She hadn't seen him since yesterday when she delivered a message to Bruce during the afternoon staff meeting. Bruce left the meeting early and hadn't come back to the office since.

Jake left his name, thanked her, and turned onto Memorial Drive. He called Drummond's house. When the machine answered, Jake said, "Good thing you're not home, Drum. I'm in a cranky mood. Call me when you want to tell the truth—Vicki Shaw included."

Jake put down the phone feeling no better. He cut through a couple of back streets to Avon, where he backed into a parking space. He shut off the engine and opened the car door.

Watson pranced along Martin Street toward the fourth-floor apartment he shared with Jake. The black dog waited at the outer door until Jake opened it and let Watson into the foyer, where Jake opened the metal mailbox. It was always filled when he'd spent the night with Gloria. Today was no exception.

Mail in hand, Jake opened the inner door onto an off-white painted lobby. Watson bolted up ahead, stopping at each landing while Jake, glancing at his mail, climbed steadily but slowly.

Inside his apartment, Jake tossed the mail onto his desk, freshened Watson's water, and got a beer for himself. The printed page he'd taken from Vicki's desk was burning a hole in his pocket. He sat in the living room, took out the paper, and read:

> On a murder map of connect the dots, the shape is triangular, starting with Boston on June 14, 1962, moving north to Lynn, then northeast to Salem, where witches burned. On November 23, 1963, the tenth victim was found in Lawrence, eighteen miles west.
>
> Two sides of the triangle were complete. The third side connects Lawrence to Boston with a stop in Cambridge, where Beverly Samans was raped and strangled. A knife was used on her as well. The last victim, the thirteenth, was found on January 4, 1964, in an apartment on Charles Street three blocks from Boston Common. Ten months later, on November 5, a man known as the Boston Strangler was arrested.
>
> However, the man arrested was the wrong man. Bad enough on its own but made worse by the fact that the police in charge of the investigation knew that the real killer was still at large.

Jake put down the page. It was one thing to have listened to Drummond talk about the possibility of a police conspiracy, quite another to read the charges in print. Somehow, seeing the words on paper gave them a greater meaning, a reality for Jake that they'd never had before. It was a reality, however, that he didn't want to believe; it was like being told after the tenth test that there is no doubt, you do have cancer.

What shape of noose was Drummond sticking his neck into? Jake wondered and dialed Drummond's home. No answer. It wasn't unusual for Drummond not to answer when he was busy writing. Jake imagined him at his computer, tuning out the world. But not for long, Jake thought, then punched in another number. In seconds, he got through to Lieutenant Dane.

"This is Jake. I know you don't want me butting in, Tommy, but this is important. I've got something you ought to see."

"What is it?"

"A page of manuscript," Jake said, remembering the two cops carrying boxes out of Ruth Hill's apartment. "My guess is, it's part of the manuscript your men removed from Hill's desk. I think you should see it."

Dane agreed to meet at Rocco's Deli, a local dive over the Tobin Bridge in Chelsea. Jake sat at the lunch counter absently stirring a cup of black coffee with a plastic swizzle stick. Outside, semis pulled in and out of a giant produce warehouse. Down the road, junk cars and scrap metal were being loaded on a freighter for a ride to Japan. In six months, they'd roll off cargo ships somewhere in America as Toyotas or Hondas.

Tommy Dane swung his unmarked car into the adjacent empty lot and parked next to Jake's worn Saab. When he opened the door and got out, Watson poked his head through the Saab's open window, a sign of acknowledgment that Dane ignored. Disappointed, Watson sat back down as the lieutenant walked quickly inside.

"Coffee?" the waitress asked, the pot in her hand.

Dane sat on the stool beside Jake, nodding to the waitress. "Cream. One sugar," he said, watching the cup fill, the steam rise. When she finished, Dane turned to Jake. "What's this all about?" he asked impatiently.

"You tell me. You're the one keeping all the secrets."

"I don't have time for games, Jake."

Jake put the manuscript page on the counter. Dane read it, emotionless.

"Where'd you get this?" he asked.

"I paid a visit to Vicki Shaw's apartment."

"You broke in?" Dane snapped.

"Her roommate was there," Jake said. "I borrowed the page when I left."

Dane pushed the paper in front of Jake, then took a cigarette from his pack. He lit it, filling his lungs with one long pull. He blew out grayish smoke. "I appreciate the tip, Jake. But what is it you think you've got here?"

"Part of a book Bruce Drummond is writing. I don't know the details, but from what I gather, Ruth Hill and Vicki Shaw were somehow involved."

"Hill was the typist," Dane said, tapping the ash of his cigarette in the tray. "What she was typing was a trash book. A pack of lies about a case long-ago solved."

Jake made no judgment. "And Vicki Shaw?" he asked.

"As far as we can tell from the pages we removed from Hill's apartment, Vicki was writing the book with Drummond." Dane cut Jake a look. "We're trying to find her to verify that. Any idea where she is?"

Jake shook his head. "None," he said, adding that Drummond had told him he was writing something big.

"Writing a big lie is more like it," Dane said, looking steadily at Jake. "That's why I was disappointed when I heard you were working for him. Has Drummond got you convinced that the Strangler investigation was dirty?"

Jake answered with a question of his own. "Was it?"

Dane nodded. "In the mind of crackpot writers," he said without emotion. "Drummond's been scratching the Strangler itch for years. I never figured he'd draw you into it, Jake."

"How about you, Tommy?" Jake asked. "How deeply are you drawn into it?"

"What's that supposed to mean?" Dane said, bristling.

"I mean that whether I want to believe in a police cover-up or not, I can't ignore that women are being raped and strangled and that Drummond is talking loudly about the real Strangler's return."

Dane took a deep, angry drag on his cigarette. "Drummond needs to sell newspapers," he said dismissively.

Jake shook his head. "It won't wash, Tommy. Drummond kept all this out of his paper so he could hit the big time with the biggest secret of his life. Besides, it's not just Drum. It's Vicki Shaw, too. How do you explain her involvement?"

"Who says I have to?"

"Just answer the question, Tommy. Why would a bright Harvard graduate student get mixed up with Bruce Drummond if all he were telling was a pack of lies?"

"You seem to have the answers," Dane said cuttingly. "You tell me."

"I can't," Jake admitted. "But I think you and I should go have a nice long talk with Drummond. You already know he's my client. I've nothing to hide. It'll clear the air around this mess. What do you say?"

"I say I'd take you up on it, Jake, but like Miss Shaw, Bruce Drummond seems to have dropped out of sight."

"What are you talking about?" Jake asked, his pulse quickening.

"Drummond's disappeared. I wanted to speak with him about a few things myself. Can't find him anywhere." Dane rubbed out his cigarette, then got up from the counter. "This manuscript has a lot of people nervous, Jake. It's like playing with fire. I wouldn't want to see Drummond or Miss Shaw get burned."

Jake met Dane's stare. "The way Ruth Hill did, you mean?" Jake asked. "Is her connection to that manuscript why she was murdered?"

Dane turned. "Take care, Jake," he said. "Don't you get too close to the fire either."

"Tommy . . . ?"

Dane was not answering.

Chapter 9

The big man swung open the wire gate and released the dogs. He closed the gate, then latched it. He wiped his sweaty palms across his pants, glad the dogs were safely locked inside.

He checked his watch. Just after two. Plenty of time, he thought, fighting back his irritation. He liked being in command, in complete control. Since coming back to Boston, however, he felt that something was controlling him: a manuscript and the people associated with it. There was little he could do about the words on a page, but he knew how to deal with the Ruth Hills of the world.

Dealing with a man was a different matter. He had never killed a man before. Never given it any thought. In his youth hampered by his own anxieties and psychological impediments, he had little to do with the boys he went to private school with in Boston. They bored him with box scores and ball games. The games he played, he kept to himself.

They wouldn't believe him anyway. Like the dead animals in the biology lab. It wasn't a cruel prank performed by some disgruntled older kid. He did it for the simple reason he wanted to know what it felt like to take a life. Lab life would die anyway. It was in the lab to experiment on.

And now, all these years later, Drummond was a new experiment. The big man created something special for the reporter responsible for writing the manuscript.

He looked back at the dogs, a dark ache swelling inside him as his heart beat faster.

The only thing to do now was wait.

Watson had his muzzle out the partially opened car window sniffing the salty air. A wall of gray clouds bringing a cold autumn rain was off to the east. Jake cranked up the Saab's heater and switched the fan to high, warding off the worst chill on earth: thirty-two degrees with a northeast wind bringing rain in off the ocean. When the first drops hit the windshield, Jake reached across the seat and cranked Watson's window closed. Watson barked his disapproval.

"Sorry, old pal," Jake said, his thoughts troubled. Where the hell is Drummond? he wondered. Off with the also-missing Vicki Shaw? Working in secret on another chapter of the manuscript while I hunt for answers on my own? Even Dane won't offer the time of day. "We're being ignored," Jake said to Watson, who still sulked about the closed window. "I stand corrected," Jake muttered. "I'm being ignored."

Jake picked up the car phone and called Drummond's office. Bruce still hadn't been in. Jake put down the phone and headed for Boston's South End, where Drummond owned a house.

The sky had partially cleared by the time Jake turned down Warren Avenue and parked illegally in a spot reserved for residents. He cracked open a window for Watson, then got out and walked toward the four-story brownstone on the corner of West Canton. Drummond had lived in the South End for thirty years and in this house for twenty. Since his wife died five years ago, he'd lived alone in the huge house except for the occasional out-of-town visit from one of his adult children.

Jake stood at the massive double door, rapping the brass knocker for entry. He waited, then knocked again, this time harder. Still nothing.

He peered into the living room window looking for some sign that Drummond was on his way. He got no sign and tried the door. A shiver ran down Jake's spine when it swung open easily.

Jake stepped into the hall. The eerie silence was broken only by the sound of a mantel clock ticking over the marble fireplace.

"Drum?" Jake shouted up the stairs. "Bruce? Hello?"

When no answer returned, Jake pulled his revolver, wishing like hell Watson were with him. He thought of going back to get his partner but proceeded on his own to check the floors above.

Raindrops hit against the stained-glass window as Jake climbed the stairs in the cold house. Or was the chill he felt brought on by his sense of dread that something had happened to Drummond?

"Drum? Drummond?" Jake shouted again, taking the stairs two at a time now, his .38 gripped tightly in his right hand. On the third floor, Jake worked his way down through each guest bedroom. Two were unused, the beds neatly made. The third had had a recent guest.

Jake opened drawers and checked out the closet and the adjoining bath. On the shower rack, Jake found some Paul Mitchell shampoo and mousse. Definitely not Bruce's. Jake went back to the bedroom for a closer look. In the wastebasket were tissues used to blot lipstick. Vicki Shaw's? Jake wondered, continuing his search.

On the second floor, the television room showed more signs of reading than watching. Magazines and old newspapers were piled around a large, well-used recliner. Still no sign of Drummond.

Jake went through the master bedroom, impressed with the neatness. He'd expected Drummond to be messy, but the rooms in general showed signs of a man nearly compulsive about picking up after himself.

Back on the first floor, Jake called Bruce's name once again, then went through the living room and into the study. On the massive oak desk beside the computer workstation was a neatly stacked pile of manuscript pages. Jake hesitated, the hairs on the back of his neck bristling.

He looked behind him, hoping Drummond had instantly appeared. When he hadn't, Jake picked up the printout and read it.

The Strangler imagined faces inside the house looking out at him. He turned away, glancing at his watch. It was four o'clock, June 14. His first victim was about to die.

He looked behind him. Nothing but the sounds of heavy traffic moving out of Boston. He crossed the street and slipped between parked cars when the woman he'd been waiting for came down the street. She was small, back bent with age. Her short gray hair framed warm, pleasant eyes, a generous smile.

Her name was Anna Slessers. She carried two small bags of groceries. She lived at 77 Gainsborough Street, apartment 3F on the front. She worked until three each day, then stopped to shop before coming home at four.

It was the same every day. A regimented life so predictable that she bored him even though he was about to kill her.

He flattened his thick hair with the palm of his hand, then pulled his Red Sox cap low over his forehead so people passing couldn't see the restlessness in his eyes. He smiled to himself and glanced again at his watch. Only a few minutes had passed.

Don't hurry, he told himself and climbed the outside steps behind her. His smile broadened, his eyes warmed so she wouldn't be frightened as she looked at him. He reached out to the door for her. He took one of her bags, a true gentleman. He was toying with her, but what was the point of premeditated crime if you couldn't enjoy it, play with it?

He pulled the door closed behind him and followed her in.

Attached to the page was a hand-written note. Jake recognized the writing as Drummond's. The note read, "Vicki, as you can see from this copy, I'm experimenting with a 'you-are-there' approach. I think it adds excitement but am concerned that it may damage our credibility. It may also present a problem dovetailing with the sections you're drafting. The question is, how far can/should we push this? Read the new sections. Let's discuss them later. If you don't like them, we can always have Ruthie retype." Drummond's initials ended the note.

When Jake put back the note, a scrap of torn fax paper caught his attention. The message had been sent to Drummond. "Talkative women say you are trying to ruin my family. I'll give you the chance to prove otherwise, and—perhaps—the interview of your life. Bring what you've written along with coauthor, Vicki Shaw (didn't I say talkative women?) to me at a time and place coming later. Be there."

Jake's insides knotted as he searched the desk for the time and place. He found nothing except Drummond's notebook. He flipped through it to the last page. It had been torn out.

Jake turned on the desk lamp. He held the blank top page near the bulb and saw the heavy impression that a pencil or pen had left. Jake dug around for a pencil. Lightly, he shaded around the impression until he could read a series of directions. He copied them, switched out the light, and hurried to his car.

Boston is a uniquely small town in many ways, but it's like every other big city during rush hour. Cars line up for miles to crawl in at eight in the morning, then back out at five in the afternoon. Ebb and flow, just like the tide. A million cars go in, a million cars come out. It's programmed insanity, but it works.

On this late afternoon, however, it was working slower than usual. The forty-minute ride to the bedroom community of Townsend, north of the city, took sixty minutes before Jake hit the edge of town.

From there, Jake followed the directions found on Drummond's pad to Harrison's Farm Rental. He turned left and drove for two miles, crossed a small bridge, and turned off onto a dirt road. A half mile down was another road on the right. According to the directions, Drummond and Vicki Shaw were to meet someone one hundred yards up that road.

But for what? The question clawed at Jake's insides as he pulled onto the loose shoulder and parked. In a ditch below, curled feathers spun on brackish, still water. Jake let Watson out, then started through the woods that paralleled the narrow road. Watson worked the ground in front, watching for the slightest movement, listening for the faintest sound. The fall frost had killed the once-thick growth, making the going easy in the failing afternoon sun.

Seventy yards ahead, Jake saw a small, unkempt shack. Behind it, angling up a slight grade, was a row of chain-link dog pens. Watson's ears wicked back and forth like a horse sensing oncoming rain.

Jake pulled his Smith & Wesson, then picked up the pace through the tree cover. At the beginning of the road, he stopped. Car tracks had flattened the grass that grew in the gravelly ruts. Jake signaled Watson forward, then followed him into a clearing bordered on one side by scrub and thorny bushes studded with red berries. Raindrops clung to the berries like so many rubies. Parked behind the thickest branches, so inconspicuous that Jake nearly missed it, was Drummond's Buick.

Jake's pulse quickened as he moved toward the car. The driver's-side window was open, the driver's seat wet from the rain. Jake opened the door, his attention drawn to a wadded ball of paper on the floor mat. He picked it up and opened it. It was the original set of directions to the kennel that Jake had found on Drummond's desk. Added to it in pencil was the meeting time: 2:30.

Jake glanced at his watch. The meeting was over an hour ago. That Drummond's car was still here was a bad sign for both Drum and Vicki Shaw. Jake closed the car door, his attention on Watson, who was stalking forward apprehensively. Suddenly, the stout dog stopped, then lowered himself to the ground. He let out a deep, throaty growl followed by a nervous licking of his chops. Jake's eyes followed the dog's fixed stare.

Two emaciated Dobermans were locked inside the kennel runs, circling like zoo animals wanting freedom. When they saw Jake, their necks stiffened and arched back, showing a pinkish tint to their ferocious eyes. They skittered backward, snarling fiercely.

Quickly, one after the other, they hurled themselves against the fence with savage, throat-high attacks. For a moment, their claws gripped the chain link. They held and fell back with hate-filled eyes, then attacked again.

It was when they were both in the air that Jake saw the man's body. He was in the back corner of the pen, as far away from the dogs as possible. His clothes were ripped, exposing huge, bloody gouges of missing flesh. The man was obviously dead, but the means of his death made Jake's stomach tighten and fall away into some painful lightness.

Jake moved closer, then stopped. His stomach rolled into nausea when he saw that the dead man was Bruce Drummond—the tough, old newspaperman who was deathly afraid of dogs.

Jake wanted to look away, but his job, his duty was to look for Vicki Shaw. He swallowed back the bitter, rising bile and made himself search the grounds, made himself do the job he was hired to do.

The sad fact, however, was that Drummond hadn't let him do it. Drummond hadn't let go. Now Drum lay before him, the horrible shock of death riveted to his face.

The only consolation—there was no sign of Vicki Shaw.

Chapter 10

"Did you see da paper, Jake?" Carmine was cutting open bundles of the morning's Boston *Herald*. A close-up photo of two wild-eyed dobermans looked out from the page. "Dogs! They ate 'im!"

Jake counted out the change and set it on the counter. Rosie closed the lid on a cup of black coffee. She scooped up the change. "No paper this morning, Jake?" Concern laced her voice. The mother of the neighborhood sensed his pain. "What iz it, Jake? Too much people kilt, eh? I said the very same to Carmine, too much people kilt. And now de dogs." Rosie's chin knotted, her mouth turned down. "Iz terrible."

Jake nodded agreement, turned up his collar, and stepped into the north wind. The first dusting of snow this season was ripping in on an early Canadian express due to arrive later in the day. Jake felt the chill in his bones and wondered what happened to the warm days of Indian summer. He bent at the waist, leaning into the wind. Watson, head held high, ears blown back, trotted alongside. It was nine in the morning. Jake had spent a troubled night after driving back to Boston in a stupor. He'd called the state police to report Drummond's death, then waited an hour for someone to arrive on the scene. The trooper was one of those massive-necked types, cut from stone with a matching grim expression. He asked Jake a hundred questions while waiting for the two-man contingent from the Humane Society to tranquilize and remove the dogs. He asked Jake fifty questions more as the medical examiner examined the body.

Drummond died of fright or from loss of blood. Either way, the dogs killed him.

On the drive back to Cambridge, Jake couldn't rid himself of the gruesome fact that Drummond was terrified of dogs. He was lured to that abandoned kennel and deliberately tortured. Who knew enough about Drummond to do such a thing? And why? What horrifying thoughts must have gone through his old friend's mind when he realized what was about to happen? And further, what had become of Vicki Shaw?

These questions kept Jake tossing most of the night. When he did fall asleep, his dreams were a mixture of attacking dobermans and one panicked man crying out for help that never came.

At the corner of Martin Street, Jake turned into his apartment complex. He opened the door for Watson, then followed him up the stairs. His office phone was ringing as he unlocked the door.

"Yes?"

"Jake Eaton?" It was the voice of a woman in a panic. "I saw the pictures in the morning papers."

The anxious voice was unsettling. "Who is this?" Jake asked.

"Vicki Shaw. Drummond said I could trust you. I need help." The voice cracked through a gush of air. "Please. I don't know who else to call."

Newport, Rhode Island, has a natural cycle like a flower: it wakes up in spring, blossoms in summer, fades in fall, and sleeps in winter. It possesses a lovely harbor, cliff walks, and gorgeous mansions. It also held a very scared Vicki Shaw hiding out in a bed-and-breakfast on Thames Street.

Jake pulled into the gravel parking lot and got out. He climbed the wooden stairs to the porch, told Watson to stay, and went inside. Vicki's room was on the second floor. Jake hadn't knocked when the door opened. Before him stood a slender woman in her thirties with dark chestnut hair falling around her face. Her arms were crossed tightly as if she were cold. The place was anything but cold.

"Jake Eaton?"

"That's right," Jake said, thinking how young and frightened she seemed.

She made no sign of inviting Jake inside. "Bruce said you have an unusual partner."

"A dog."

"Where is he?" she asked, her dark eyes tracking the hall.

"In the car."

"He has an unusual name."

"Watson."

She stepped back. Jake entered the room, closing the door behind him. Vicki brushed back her hair with one trembling hand, exposing a thin face with rich brown eyes made red from crying. She wore a blue-and-black-checked flannel shirt and black jeans. She shoved her hands in her jeans pockets, not trying to diguise the fear that suddenly left her speechless.

Jake went to the window. He pulled back the lace curtain and looked out onto the street below. It was quiet, empty—just like the harbor. Over Goat Island, a moutain of dark clouds boiled in the sky. Jake turned back to Vicki, but she spoke first.

"Were the papers right?" she asked, her forehead shiny with perspiration. "Was it Bruce?"

"It was."

Her eyes clamped shut. "I told him not to play cops and robbers with this," she said, her eyes steady on Jake. "I warned him that some people would do anything to keep this secret buried, but Bruce wouldn't listen. He was like a child with a new toy. He was fascinated by the possibility of discovering the truth after all these years."

"The truth about the Boston Strangler?" Jake asked.

Vicki's eyes stayed steady on Jake. "I thought Bruce explained everything when he came to see you about Ruth Hill. Didn't he?"

Jake shook his head. "Drummond explained very little," he said. "He was particularly evasive about his source—some might say his partner in writing a certain book. That would be you, wouldn't it?"

Vicki nodded slightly. "Yes," she admitted, taking a seat on the edge of the bed. She rested her hands on the mattress as if to steady herself. "We wanted to keep our collaboration quiet."

"From whom?"

"Everyone except a trusted few. Bruce said his years as a reporter had taught him to keep his work-in-progress close to the vest."

"Why?"

"Because reporters are thieves," Vicki said. "They'd steal our story."

"Maybe, but they wouldn't kill for it."

"No," Vicki said, driving her fists down into the bed in frustration. "I can't believe this is happening," she blurted.

"That's a good place to start, Miss Shaw. It *is* happening. And if experience tells me anything, it's likely to get worse before it gets better." Jake met her sad gaze and spoke directly. "The killer's likely to come after you next."

Vicki closed her eyes and pulled in a long, deep breath. It released in jerks.

Jake asked her about the fax that Drummond received regarding the Townsend meeting.

"Yes, I saw it," Vicki said. "That's when I came down here. Bruce brought me, then went to the meeting on his own."

"Why didn't he call me for help?" Jake asked, his own frustration showing. "He must've known the risk he was taking."

"He didn't ask for help because we didn't think there was any danger," Vicki said.

"We?" The word hung in the air accusingly.

"Yes, we," Vicki spit back. "Bruce thought the Strangler had made contact."

"A vicious killer had made contact," Jake corrected her, the idea of Drummond going up against a professional killer making his head pound. Jake couldn't contain himself. "If there was no danger, why did Drummond drive you a hundred miles in the opposite direction? It doesn't make sense."

Vicki's eyes widened. "It might if you listened!" She glared at Jake. "I've studied serial killers for years. They don't change. They kill in the same way. Always. The man Bruce went to meet—the man he believed to be the Boston Strangler—has a history of rape and strangulation as his modus operandi. His behavioral profile suggests that he would not kill a man. It was inconceivable. The danger would have been to me, not Bruce. That's why I came down here and Bruce went along on his own."

"So what happened?" Jake asked, his voice still edgy. "What put Drummond in the morgue?"

The question seemed deflating. Vicki's eyes lost their fire. "I don't know," she admitted, then sagged as if an emotional weight was too great for her. "*I* told Bruce there was little danger in his going to that meeting. *I* told Bruce a man would have nothing to fear. *I* sent him into that pen with killer dogs!" Vicki said, then broke into sobs. She closed her eyes, not bothering to cover her pale face and twisted mouth. The tears fell freely.

The image of Drummond's ghastly death sapped Jake of any patience or tenderness. It even prevented consolation. He turned away from the poor girl and asked coolly, "Did Drummond take the manuscript with him to Townsend?"

"Some of it," Vicki said. "We worked independently for the most part. We'd get together and combine our efforts once a week or so. Bruce took with him what pages he had when he went to meet the Strangler. Why?"

"Motive," Jake said, thinking out loud. "If the Boston Strangler has come back and added Drummond to his list of victims, he did so for a purpose."

"The manuscript?"

"It would seem so," Jake said. "Do you have any of it?"

Vicki nodded slightly. "Yes." She pointed to the laptop computer on the bureau. "It's in there."

Jake stepped to the closet and picked up a travel bag. "Come on Miss Shaw, you can't stay here," he said.

"I can't go back to my place," she said. "I don't know where—"

"We'll think of something," Jake said, helping her up. "Bring your computer and let's get out of here." His uneasiness was gaining strength.

It was an uneasiness brought on by the possibility that the Strangler was back and more unpredictable than ever. Or that another killer was out there driven by the need to stop a manuscript from ever being completed.

Neither option made Jake's job any easier. Now that job was to keep Vicki Shaw alive.

Chapter 11

A light snow began falling on the drive back to Boston. The flakes were small, driven horizontally by the north wind. When enough collected on the windshield, Jake flicked on the wipers. He'd just turned them off when Vicki leaned back in the seat, letting out a sigh.

Jake had left her alone with her thoughts before asking about being a graduate student at Harvard. Vicki wasn't very talkative. Jake drove a few more miles in silence. In the back, Watson nosed the window, making designs on the glass.

Jake tried at conversation. "I spoke to your roommate," he said. "She mentioned you hadn't found your work at Harvard easy going."

"Jan said that?" There was a hint of surprise in Vicki's soft voice. "I didn't know she was that insightful," she said, then immediately regretted it. "I'm sorry. Jan's a good person to share space with. We're different, that's all." She glanced at Jake. "Did she tell you the nature of my troubles?" she asked.

"She mentioned the Ebberhardt Institute," Jake said. "Jan said you'd been locked out."

Vicki forced a smile. "That's a bit oversimplified, but it amounted to the same thing. My research focuses on women serial killers. To understand how they differ from men, I wanted to study men serials first. Professor Ebberhardt had a lot of trouble granting me free access to that data."

"Did he give a reason?" Jake asked.

"Only after I demanded one. Then it really didn't address the issue. Not to me, at least." Vicki sat up straight in her seat. "Professor Ebberhardt said I was admitted to the graduate program to research women serials—which is true. I was, he put plainly, to *stay* with that topic. There was no more room for research regarding male serials." Again Jake flicked on the wipers. "What's one more student doing one more study?" he asked, failing to see the point.

"Everything," Vicki said, explaining that researchers stake out informational domains much the same as miners stake out land claims. "I was granted my space, and I was to stay in it."

"But you didn't."

"No, I didn't," Vicki said without apology.

Watson shifted position in the backseat, yawned, then curled up, resting his head on one of Vicki's bags. Jake shifted the conversation just as easily.

"Tell me about Ruth Hill," Jake said. "Was she helping you with your research in some way?"

Vicki's expression showed surprise. "Harvard would frown on that," she said. "How'd you know?"

Jake flashed her a slight smile. "I'm a private detective, Miss Shaw—"

"Vicki, please."

Jake nodded. "I'm a private detective, Vicki. I'm paid to know things people like to keep quiet. Ruth was employed by the university to work on the final draft of your dissertation, yet according to Drummond she spent some of her time doing research. How'd that come about?"

"Quite simply, really," Vicki admitted, explaining that once Professor Ebberhardt denied her access to the data she needed from the institute, she decided to go after the information the old-fashioned way: dig. Vicki spent her time at the Boston Public Library while Ruth—familiar with newspaper offices—scoured the paper's file copies. "That's how I came to meet Drummond," Vicki added.

"Ruth put you two together?"

"Yes. Bruce was like a little kid when he found out that my research had veered off into an investigation of the 1960s Boston Strangler case. It didn't take long for him to propose that we look into it together," Vicki said, growing somber. "Big mistake."

The mistake, Jake knew, would be to bog down in the emotions of Drummond's murder. You have to work through them, beat them back. He was determined not to let Vicki stop and sink.

"Drummond had been interested in the Strangler case for years," Jake prompted. "Something would catch his attention every now and then, but he never managed to get it all down on paper. You were probably a stimulus for him."

"I think that's a fair statement," Vicki said. "After talking things over for a while, we started working together on the draft of a book."

"I saw it," Jake told her. "I borrowed a page from your apartment when I spoke with Jan."

"Borrowed?" There was a hint of playfulness in Vicki's question.

"You can have it back. It's at my place. I think you should stay there for a few days until I come up with a better idea."

"All right," Vicki said, and her mood once again sank. "I don't know how I can pay you."

"Don't worry about it."

"But I do."

"Drummond paid in advance," Jake said, then shifted the conversation back to the Strangler and Vicki's interest in a murder investigation more than thirty years old.

"I wasn't interested at first," Vicki answered, then explained how that changed.

To study women killers, she needed to establish a baseline for comparison to men killers. The Ebberhardt Institute has the most complete database in the world pertaining to men serial killers. So Vicki began by analyzing the educations, family backgrounds, criminal histories, and several other demographic factors available on all men serial killers.

"You were wandering out of your space," Jake said knowingly.

Vicki nodded. "I was. And," she continued, "I wandered into something fascinating: Albert DeSalvo—the man identified and jailed as the Strangler—did not fit the behavior profile of a serial killer."

Jake took his eyes off the road for longer than normal. "He what?" he asked, looking at her.

"My examination of all the records indicates that DeSalvo could not have been the Boston Strangler," she said without a hint of doubt.

"You can prove that?" Jake asked.

"I already have," Vicki answered slyly. "Once Bruce found that out from Ruth, he came knocking."

"I'm surprised he didn't tear down your door," Jake mused. "But if DeSalvo wasn't the Strangler, who was?" he asked, still not wanting to believe that a conspiracy had wormed its way into the fabric of justice. Not that it couldn't happen. Jake knew it could. That was the trouble.

Vicki shrugged slightly. "I don't know who the Strangler was," she admitted. "My research privileges at the institute were suspended before I could look into it. Bruce thought that Professor Ebberhardt suspected I was going to do just that, and—to use Jan's phrase—he locked me out."

Jake's thoughts shuttled between driving and Vicki's answers. "Did you complain to Ebberhardt about that?" Jake asked, backing off the gas pedal.

"I did," Vicki said with a hint of exasperation. "Professor Ebberhardt said I would not be making such foolish speculations if I confined my study to women, as I was supposed to."

Jake braked for the typically heavy traffic at the split on the expressway north. He gathered his thoughts, then asked how Lori Churchwell and Sylvia Reardon fit in.

Vicki began with Churchwell. She said that Lori was a student of hers in a general psychology class offered through Harvard Extension, Harvard's equivalent to a continuing education program. Extension students are mostly older working folks coming back to college to better their careers and to meet new people. Lori fit the pattern: she was a forty-eight-year-old divorced mother of two grown children. She'd been employed at Tower Records as the events organizer for band promotions. Most importantly, she was bored.

"Lori," Vicki added, "found the course material interesting but not a challenge. She asked if she could do something extra, something outside of class. I said she could do some fieldwork for me."

Jake eased through the last of the traffic, then shifted the Saab into fifth. Boston, veiled in a late-afternoon snowy sky, lay twenty minutes ahead. He pushed Vicki for details.

"She lined up interviews mostly," Vicki said. "Bruce had a few people he wanted to speak with about DeSalvo in particular and the book in general. Lori was doing the preliminary work—locating people who had moved, contacting them to see if they'd be willing to talk to Bruce, that sort of thing."

Jake cut Vicki a surprised look. "I thought you and Drummond wanted to keep your work secret," he said.

"We did."

"Letting students help doesn't seem the best way to handle sensitive material. Why'd you take the chance?" Jake asked.

"Because we couldn't do everything on our own," Vicki answered. "We had to have some help. Besides, Lori wasn't given anything all that sensitive."

"Depends on who she spoke to," Jake explained. "If someone with something to hide got a call from her about a book you and Drummond were writing, it might have set off some alarms. Do you know who Lori phoned?"

Vicki shook her head. "I don't. That was Bruce's project. He worked on getting Lori names," she said.

"More of Drummond's quest for secrecy?"

"It wasn't that in this case," Vicki said, smiling. "Bruce liked to conduct interviews. It was the newspaperman in him. I wasn't very good at quizzing people, so Bruce worked with Lori setting up questions and contacts."

"Did Lori conduct any interviews herself?" Jake asked.

"No. At least, not with our consent."

"Meaning she might have on her own?"

Vicki nodded. "As I said, Lori wanted a challenge. She might have interviewed someone."

And gotten herself killed, Jake thought, asking what went through Vicki's mind when she'd heard Lori had been found raped and strangled.

"I was petrified," she said, her voice intense. "I demanded that Bruce and I go to the police and tell them everything," she gushed. "But Bruce wouldn't hear of it."

"Did he say why?" Jake asked.

"Bruce believed that the police might be involved somehow. Going to them, he thought, would put us in greater danger." Vicki leaned back against the headrest and rolled her eyes upward. "We kept everything to ourselves until Ruth Hill was killed," she said, her hands cupped over her face. She pulled in a steadying breath, then took her hands down. Looking at Jake, she said, "Bruce said you could help us. Can you?"

"I'm going to try," Jake said, taking the Chinatown exit toward the pike and home. He flicked the wipers to clear the snow, wishing there was a switch he could pull that would clear his thoughts just as easily.

"I don't want to die, Mr. Eaton." Vicki's voice was low, distant. It sounded as if she'd already died and was drifting slowly away. "I don't," she repeated. "I don't want to die."

Nobody does, Jake thought, giving Vicki time to catch her breath. He'd ask her about Sylvia Reardon when Vicki was better able to answer.

From the strained look in her eyes, that might be a while.

Chapter 12

While Vicki unpacked in the bedroom, Jake shopped at Evergood's, the local market. He bought a chicken, a head of bib lettuce, beets, broccoli, and cereal and milk for breakfast. Jake was not a cook—he preferred take-out and restaurants—but he did his best to make sure that Vicki had no excuse for culinary boredom. He tossed a farm-raised trout and a pound of hamburger into the basket. At the checkout counter, he grabbed bags of potato chips and cheese curls and a package of chocolate chip cookies. He knew that Watson had plenty of food and that the liquor cabinet was well supplied. What else could Vicki want? he wondered as he paid the cashier and walked back to his apartment.

He was putting away the groceries when Vicki came into the kitchen looking drawn and exhausted. "Nice place," she said, trying to sound cheery.

"I like it." Jake found an old container of Cantonese diced duck in the back of the fridge. It was one of Gloria's favorites. He put it on the floor for Watson, who eagerly dug in. "Watson's staying with you," Jake said. "He has an iron stomach. Give him whatever you don't want."

"I'm not really hungry," Vicki said, leaning against the counter. "What are you going to do?"

"I'm going to break the news to my lady friend that I'm working tonight," Jake said and closed the refrigerator. "I won't be late. Why don't you get some rest. You look beat."

"I haven't slept in a while," Vicki admitted. "I can't seem to find any peace."

"You've found it now," Jake said, deciding to hold his questions regarding Sylvia Reardon. "If you're up when I get back, we can talk then," he said, putting his coat back on. He descended the stairs and stepped into the clear, crisp night.

The afternoon's snow shower had covered gardens and garbage cans with two inches of white fluff. Jake thrived on the change of seasons, the unpredictability of East Coast weather. One day it could be sixty degrees, the next day below freezing. He thought that weathermen and private investigators were a lot alike; both survey the elements, then hazard educated guesses. But, just now, Jake felt that a storm had unsuspectedly crept up on him.

All he knew for certain was that Drummond's killer had set a trap that Vicki Shaw managed to avoid. He knew that the killer wanted their manuscript, the existence of which likely became known to him through Lori Churchwell's phone calls. Had Ruth Hill in her research efforts also tipped off someone? A cop, maybe? Someone connected to Harvard? Or perhaps a rival newsman? Was it time for an educated guess? No way, Jake thought, turning onto Hanover Street.

It was past eight before Jake met Gloria for dinner in Boston's Italian North End. He squeezed his way through the well-dressed bar crowd and over to their usual corner table, where Gloria sat waiting. She wore a dark green cashmere sweater over a white silk blouse open at the neck. From her ears dangled large silver star-shaped earrings that caught the candlelight like beacons.

"I was afraid you'd forgotten," she said, reaching out and taking Jake's hand. "I know you've got more important things to think about. It was terrible about Drummond. I'm so sorry, Jake."

Jake bent and kissed her on the cheek. He sat across from her, moving a vase of flowers to one side to see her more clearly. The waiter came and placed oversized menus before them. Gloria ordered another scotch. Jake asked for a vodka gimlet, light on the lime, heavy on the vodka. When the waiter left, Gloria asked Jake how he managed to get through last night.

"A little rough, but it was all right," Jake said, appreciating her concern.

"You should have come down to the boat."

"And kept you awake? One of us was enough," Jake said. "I won't be much company tonight, either. I've got Drummond's partner in my apartment for a few days."

Gloria's eyebrows raised a fraction. "I didn't know he had one," she said.

"I mentioned her. Vicki Shaw," Jake said, jarring her memory about the book that Bruce and Vicki were working on.

Gloria seemed more interested in something else. "What does Watson think about a woman staying in your apartment?" she asked with mild reproach.

"Other than you, you mean?" Jake said, absently turning his butter knife. "Truth is, I don't think Watson minds at all. I know I don't. I guess that only leaves you," Jake said playfully. "Two out of three ain't bad."

Gloria's chin jutted forward in denial. "I don't know what you're talking about," she said.

"I'm talking about you and the unusual signs of jealousy. I'm flattered," Jake said, "but you don't have to worry. I'm as loyal to you as Watson is to me. And," he said, placing his hand in hers, "I prefer it that way. My interest in Vicki Shaw is business only."

Gloria's smile brightened. "I'll accept that," she said, "if you tell me what she's like."

The waiter brought the drinks and left. Jake took the first satisfying sip. He put down the glass and leaned back in his seat.

"That's hard to say," he admitted. "Right now she's feeling guilty as hell regarding Drummond's murder. She's supposed to be an expert in serial killers and, on her advice, Drummond walked into a cage full of dogs."

Gloria winced.

"Sorry. All I can say for sure about Vicki Shaw is that she's in a great deal of danger," Jake said, explaining Vicki's call, his drive to Newport, and his decision to keep her under wraps for a few days.

"So she's not just Drummond's partner, she's now a client," Gloria said mostly to herself.

"Adopted," Jake said. "I figure I owe Drummond that much. It's not every day I let a client walk into a death trap."

Gloria shook her head in jerks. "Don't, Jake. Now you sound like the one who's feeling guilty as hell. You can't blame yourself. Did Drummond ask you to go with him?"

"He should have, but he didn't."

"Then what could you have done? I'll tell you: nothing. You don't have a crystal ball."

"If I did, I'd be using it right now," Jake said, reaching for a nagging thought just beyond him.

"What is it?" Gloria asked.

"Something about Drummond's killer that I can't figure out," Jake said, looking into Gloria's eyes. "You sure you want to listen to this?"

"If it will help."

Jake sipped his gimlet. "It's this whole business about serial killers," he said. "Years before I met you, I worked a serial case and learned a little about how they approach killing."

Gloria sat back, a quizzical expression on her face as if Jake were speaking a foreign language. "Hold on a second," she said. "What's a serial killer have to do with Drummond? Besides, I've never heard of one using dogs as a weapon."

"That's just the point," Jake said.

"Then I'm afraid the point eludes me," Gloria said. "Care to back up?"

"Gladly," Jake said, appreciative of her interest. He knew the value of kicking around ideas, hoping that one of them would sail through the goalpost. "To begin with, a serial killer doesn't kill because he's involved in a criminal enterprise. That is, he doesn't kill as a result of robbing a bank, say. Or a family dispute turned violent. He kills for personal reasons all his own."

"Go on," Gloria asked, sipping her drink.

"His killing—in most cases—involves some sort of ritual, an acting out of some fantasy. That ritual is as much a part of the killing as is the cause of death," Jake said. "And you're right about the dogs. I've never heard of any killer using them as a weapon. Certainly, the Boston Strangler didn't."

"Did the Strangler have a ritual?" Gloria asked.

"If I remember correctly, he tied colored bows around his victim's necks after he murdered them."

Gloria's nose wrinkled. "Ghastly," she murmured.

"This whole damn business is," Jake said, getting back to the issue at hand. "Drummond went to Townsend thinking he was meeting the Strangler. He was convinced he was in no danger precisely because the Strangler's modus operandi involved the rape and strangling of women."

Gloria winced at the thought. "You're right, Jake. This is terrible business. All of it."

"Want me to stop?" Jake asked. When Gloria shook her head, Jake continued, "Let's say for a moment that the killer wasn't the Strangler."

"That would seem to make sense, because he changed his spots and killed a man," Gloria said.

Jake nodded. "That's what I thought until I started analyzing the motive more closely."

"And what do you believe the motive to be?" Gloria asked.

"The manuscript. Drummond was to take it with him."

"Again, that makes sense," Gloria said.

"Why?" Jake said, playing devil's advocate.

Gloria shrugged. "Isn't it obvious? Something in the manuscript was a threat," Gloria said. "Maybe after all these years, Drummond figured out who the real Strangler was and wrote about it."

Jake waved his index finger. "You're making the case that the killer was the Boston Strangler, not someone else."

Gloria thought a moment. "You're right," she said. "Sorry."

"That's all right. I got stuck there myself, and on one other point."

"Which is?"

Jake sipped more of his gimlet. "The killer knows about modern technology. He even faxed Drummond the note about the Townsend meeting."

"So?"

"So, with copying machines and computer disks available everywhere, why would the killer assume he could get his hands on every copy of that manuscript?"

Gloria's eyes popped wider. "Good question, Jake. Why would he?"

"I don't think he reasonably could."

"And where does that take you?" Gloria asked.

"To the possibility of another motive."

"Which is?"

Jake shook his head. "I don't know yet. But whatever it was, it led to Bruce Drummond's murder."

"And your need to protect Vicki Shaw."

"That about covers it," Jake said, then reached out and again took Gloria's hand in one of his. "But it doesn't matter. If the killer's the Boston Strangler, or someone else, I want the man who did that to Drummond. He won't get away," Jake said, picking up the menu with the other hand even though he had no appetite.

Chapter 13

Jake let Watson in after his night run, then locked the apartment door behind him. He took off his coat and unstrapped his shoulder holster. When he stepped into his office to hang up both, he saw Vicki seated at his desk, a laptop computer opened in front of her.

"I couldn't sleep," Vicki said.

"Must be going around," Jake answered, putting his revolver on the desk. "What's up? Besides you."

Vicki managed a short smile. "How was dinner?"

"Not as good as the company." Jake hung his coat in the closet thinking what little he could tell Gloria about the woman in front of him. When he turned back to Vicki, he asked her about her path to Harvard.

"Following my father's footsteps," she answered. "And his father before him. Mother went to MIT, but I never had an interest in engineering. I'm more the people type. I connect to the personal histories, not to numbers."

Jake sat across from her. "Was it a personal history that got you interested in women serial killers?"

Vicki nodded sharply. "Mine," she said. "I didn't want to be the first Shaw not to study at Harvard. I figured correctly that a proposed female study would get me in."

"And it did."

"And it did," she repeated. "By the way, I did some work while you were out. I pulled some of the DeSalvo files, thinking you'd want to begin our talk with him. I wanted to give you a hard copy, but I couldn't find your printer."

"Don't have one. Don't even have a computer," Jake admitted with a hint of pride. "It's my stand against technology. Besides, I tried computers. We didn't get along."

Vicki looked at Jake as if he'd just admitted to being from another planet. "Shall we get started?" she asked.

"By all means."

Vicki tapped a key, then focused on the screen. "Okay, let's see. Albert Henry DeSalvo: born in the Boston area, September 3, 1931. Not much of significance until the age of ten, when he started getting into trouble. By the time he was twelve," Vicki said, looking up from the screen, "he was known in the neighborhood as one of the better purse snatchers."

Jake leaned back, taking it all in.

Vicki continued. "When he was fourteen, DeSalvo was arrested on a series of breaking and enterings. A court-appointed psychiatrist evaluated him. His findings were consistent with what we know of the family history of potential serial killers."

"And that is?" Jake asked.

"Hatred of the father, a broken home, feelings of isolation, not feeling wanted or loved. Albert DeSalvo exhibited all those."

"And started stealing to get attention?" Jake wondered.

Vicki nodded. "There is a school of thought suggesting that criminals fulfill their need to be the center of attention by being caught."

"You sound skeptical."

"I am when it comes to serial killers. Their fulfillment comes from a combination of ritual and killing. That's what drives them. DeSalvo got caught stealing because DeSalvo wasn't a very good thief. In my opinion, there is nothing more to it than that."

Watson drifted in for his own dose of attention. He put his muzzle on Jake's knee and closed his eyes as Jake scratched the crown of his head.

"Go on," Jake said.

Vicki's eyes went back to the screen. "DeSalvo did odd jobs until he was seventeen," she said, as she scrolled down. "Then he got bored, lied about his age, and enlisted in the army."

"When was that?"

"That was 1948. He wound up in Germany assigned—of all places—to the military police. Apparently he liked the discipline. He achieved the rank of sergeant and was honorably discharged in 1956. By that time, he'd been married three years to a German national, Irmgard Holtzen. All I could find out about her was that she hated the United States."

Jake asked if they had children and learned there was a boy and a girl.

"The family moved back to Boston when Albert got out of the army." Vicki continued. "He seemed all right until 1958, when the records show he was arrested again on another breaking and entering. He stole some money to buy his wife a valentine and his daughter a box of candy."

"Sounds like a real tough guy," Jake said facetiously. "He's what? Thirty?"

"Twenty-seven."

"And arrested how many times?"

"At least ten."

"All on B and Es?"

"Yes," Vicki said. "But it doesn't stop there. DeSalvo was also charged once for child molestation. A little girl said DeSalvo touched her. He denied it, and the girl's mother didn't pursue it. Back in those days, few did. The charge was dropped."

Jake thought a moment. "So the guy's got a record and kinky tendencies toward the opposite sex. How does he go from stealing valentines to murdering thirteen women?"

Vicki looked approvingly at Jake. "That was exactly the question I asked," she said.

"And the answer?"

"My answer is that he didn't," she said matter-of-factly. "Not that Albert was pure. I think he was one sick man," she said, explaining one of DeSalvo's sex schemes. "He would knock on the apartment door of some unsuspecting college student and introduce himself as a talent scout for a modeling agency. His job, he told them, was to find that 'special' look."

"So?" Jake asked, as a contented Watson curled up next to his chair.

"So Albert would tell the young woman she had the qualities he was looking for. Could he, if it wasn't too much trouble, take her measurements?"

"The cover of *Vogue,* here I come," Jake surmised.

"I'm afraid so," Vicki admitted. "He'd take out his tape and rattle off a few numbers while feeling her up. There was born what the police called the Measuring Man. He did the same thing as the Green Man, only then he dressed in green maintenance coveralls. He worked his way inside on the pretense of a needed repair and again pawed the women. The cops ran a tally. They estimate he played touchy-feely more than four hundred times."

Jake's brows arched. "Four hundred?" Jake tried to imagine it. He wasn't sure he had an accurate picture when Vicki began searching the computer screen again.

She keyed in something. "Now, get this. Both the Measuring Man and the Green Man went after college-aged women. But not the Boston Strangler. Eight of the Strangler's thirteen victims were over fifty. Four were in their sixties. The oldest was eighty-five."

"That doesn't make a hell of a lot of sense," Jake said, clearly bothered. "He's doing all right with the younger set, so why move up in the age bracket?"

"Why move up and why start to kill?" Vicki asked rhetorically. "The modus operandi of the Boston Strangler was not that of Albert DeSalvo. Consider the crime scenes," she added. "Albert was a thief. Every apartment struck by the Strangler was ransacked, torn apart. Drawers were opened, clothes were thrown about, everything was gone through as part of his ritual, but nothing was taken. Any behavioral profile of DeSalvo would predict that he would take something. That's what thieves do, they steal."

Jake sat in troubled silence, digesting what Vicki had presented. "How do you explain that DeSalvo confessed?" he said finally.

"I don't," Vicki said without apology. "I don't even try. I'm a researcher. The job of a researcher is to be thorough, then to report accurately the findings. I did that. I never considered it my responsibility to identify the real Strangler. That was Bruce's passion. He lived for it."

"And it got him killed," Jake said bluntly, watching Vicki's eyes dim at the censure. Jake tried a different, kinder tack. "You may not have had Drummond's passion for finding out who the Strangler was, but you and Drum must have considered possibilities. You must have talked them out."

Vicki's eyes rested steadily on Jake. "He talked. I listened."

"And?"

A gloom seemed to take over Vicki's expression. She let out a deep, resigned sigh while her eyes scanned Jake. It was as if she was looking for his inner being, his core of strength so she could tap into it. Her eyes said she hadn't found it. She turned away. "Bruce tried to lure me into this discussion, too. I resisted."

"Why?"

"I told you," she said, her voice up a notch. "I'm a researcher, I'm not a reporter or a private detective. I'm not comfortable dealing with speculation and conjecture."

"Is that all you believed Drummond had? Speculation and conjecture?" Jake asked.

"Yes. He had no hard facts. At least he never produced any," Vicki said. "All he had was a theory that he hoped would prove itself when he went out to Townsend."

And got eaten alive, Jake thought, but he asked about the theory.

Vicki summarized it in a sentence. According to Drummond, Albert DeSalvo had been paid handsomely for his admission of guilt and the following time spent in jail.

"Remember," Vicki continued, "Massachusetts doesn't have a death penalty. According to Bruce, those who got DeSalvo into prison promised to get him out so he could spend what he'd earned by confessing."

Jake felt the muscles across his shoulders tighten. He leaned his head back and rolled it left and right to lessen the building tension. "Who were these people?" Jake asked.

"I don't know."

"How were they going to get DeSalvo out of prison?" he asked.

"I don't know that either," Vicki answered honestly. "All I know is that Bruce was looking into it with the help of Ellison Kitter."

Jake shook his head. "Who?"

"Professor Ellison Kitter," Vicki said. "He's one of the reasons I decided to study at Harvard. He's my dissertation adviser. Beyond that, I consider him a friend." She switched off the computer.

Jake asked why Drummond was talking with Professor Kitter.

"Kitter is an expert in human motivation," Vicki said. "When he was a young man, Harvard's Psychology Department was a power-house. It's still one of the tops, but nothing like it was back then."

"Why's that?"

"Because Kitter and Neil Ebberhardt had a falling out. As I understand it, they both began their academic careers in the field of human behavior. Ellison was reputed to have the better mind, Neil the better family connections and wealth. When Neil's father gave Harvard the money to build the Ebberhardt Institute, Ellison Kitter stepped into the shadows."

"Willingly?" Jake asked.

"I don't think so," Vicki admitted. "Deep down, I think Ellison resents Neil's success, but that's nothing new. Harvard is full of bitter egos."

"I think I'd like to talk to Professor Kitter."

"That's easy," Vicki said. "All you have to do is get up before the sun. He rows on the Charles River every morning." She was about to close the computer's lid when Jake stopped her.

"One second," he said. "When am I going to read your copy of the manuscript?"

"I'll print you a copy in the morning," Vicki answered. "Paper will be easier for you to read than looking at the computer screen."

"Maybe, but I don't have—"

"A printer, I know," Vicki said. "I was going to do all that at my office."

"Sorry," Jake said, rejecting that idea. "You're staying put. I'll read it off your screen if that's what I have to do. Do you have the same data in that computer that Drummond took to Townsend?"

"Everything except the chapters that Bruce gave to Lori Church-well," Vicki said. "I never had a chance to load those."

"Lori had part of your manuscript?" Jake said uneasily.

"Yes," Vicki said, trying to read Jake's expression. "I told you she was curious, eager to learn. She wanted to see what we were working on, so Bruce loaned her a few chapters for flavor. They were early drafts that we'd changed drastically. I gave them to James myself."

"Who's James?" Jake asked.

"Lori's boyfriend. Why? Is it important?"

Everything's important at this stage, Jake thought, and asked the last name of Lori's friend.

"Harper," Vicki said.

"Any idea how I might get in touch with him?"

"Now? At this hour?"

"At this hour," Jake told her and waited while Vicki produced a number from her purse. Jake picked up the phone and placed the call.

Chapter 14

Jake left his apartment with a small bat wing of discomfort flitting around in his mind. The cause was the manuscript chapters given to Lori Churchwell. Those pages led Jake to wonder if the real Strangler had learned of their existence. That's when the bat wing flapped through his frontal lobes.

The *real* Strangler? That was Drummond's mantra, not Jake's. Jake had yet to buy in to anyone's conspiracy, yet it rolled off his tongue so easily.

Time to put on the brakes, Jake thought. Hunches were one thing, proof another. And there was no proof—none that he'd seen. Maybe his trip over to O'Sheas would change that.

Tavern O'Shea was on the corner of L Street across from Holy Trinity Church in the heart of South Boston, or Southie, as the locals referred to it. Southie is neighborhood bars, a boozy brawl or two, then a quick trip to the confessional when the bars closed and the church opens. It was also the location of Tavern O'Shea, a workers' bar dating back more than a hundred years. According to the woman who answered James Harper's telephone, it was also where Jake could find the man who had lived with Lori Churchwell for the past five years.

It was almost midnight when Jake opened the tavern door and slipped through the smoky crowd to the bar. The bartender pointed toward a booth in the back. Jake bought two of what Harper had been drinking, then sauntered over to the red-haired man with a dazed look in his blue eyes.

"James Harper?" Jake asked, then introduced himself. He put the two Catamount Ales on the table and slid into the booth opposite the man. "I'd like to talk to you, if you don't mind."

"About what?" Harper asked in drunken sadness.

"Lori Churchwell."

"Well, knock me down with a feather," Harper sneered. "I never would've guessed." He glared at Jake with eyes that refused to focus. "I said all I know to the police. Now go away and leave me be," he said, flipping his hand unsteadily.

If it was a gesture for Jake to leave, it didn't take. Jake drank the foam from his glass. "I understand that the police don't have any leads," Jake said.

"Other than me, you mean," Harper said, looking worn out. "They brought me in for questioning. Domestic violence was how they intended to sweep it under the rug. Only trouble was, Lori and me never had trouble like that. Never. They couldn't make anything stick, so they finally let me go." Harper's eyes strained toward Jake. "What do you really want?" he asked.

"I'd like to help find who assaulted her, Mr. Harper. I understand she was working on a project."

Harper nodded in the stagnant tavern air. "Band promotions," he said. "Good at it, too."

"That's not the project I was referring to," Jake said. "This had to do with a class she was taking."

"Oh, that." Harper rolled his head to one side, his expression a mixture of booze and suspicion. "What's that got to do with anything?"

Jake watched Harper drain his glass, then pushed the newly bought ale in front of him. "I was hoping you could tell me," Jake said, picking at the label of his own bottle. "Do you know what Lori was doing on that project?"

"'Course I know. She was on the phone at all hours for one thing," Harper said. "Lori wanted to improve herself. She'd quit school years ago when she had her kids. The Extension School was her first try at college since then. She wanted to do well, ya know? She wanted to prove something," he said, drinking half the ale in one gulp. "One day, she brings home this manuscript and some names. Before you know it, she's making calls."

"Do you happen to remember any of those names?" Jake asked hopefully.

Harper shook his head slowly. "No," he said. "I already told the police I didn't. Doesn't matter anyway. Won't bring Lori back."

"No," Jake admitted, "but it might help me find who killed her. This is important, Mr. Harper," Jake said, trying to keep the man's attention. "Did Lori explain why she was making those calls?"

Harper shrugged. "Schoolwork," he said, studying Jake. "You go to college?"

"I did."

Harper seemed mildly disappointed. "Myself, I never finished. Not that it makes any difference. I got a good job. I got no complaints. I'm alive."

Alone in a smoky bar in South Boston wasn't exactly living, Jake thought. He asked if Harper had ever read the chapters that Bruce Drummond had given Lori.

"Those I saw, yeah. Me and Lori sat up in bed readin' 'em one night. She said we shouldn't treat it so lightly, ya know? But what the hell? It was there, ya know? You write stuff so people will read it, right?"

Right, Jake thought, thinking he'd finally gotten somewhere. "Do you remember what the chapters were about?" he asked.

Harper glared at Jake, his agitation growing. "Crazy stuff," he blurted, his face strained in concentration. "I remember what I told Lori after I read it. I said, 'Hon, you ought to give all this stuff back and let them professors have their fantasy world. Us working people don't have time for it.' She didn't pay no attention, of course." There was resentment in Harper's voice.

Jake pressed him for details. Harper sat mutely, lips pursed together, as if pondering old sorrows.

Finally, Harper said, "I went right to the police, ya know? As soon as I heard it on the news, I went right to the police and told them."

"Told them what?" Jake asked.

"About the guy mentioned in those chapters," Harper said, his patience short.

Jake leaned on the table, feeling close to the fragile edge of discovery. "What guy?" he asked.

"The lawyer, you know? What's his name?"

"Lawyer?" Jake asked, sitting upright. "DeSalvo wasn't a lawyer."

"Who said he was?" Harper asked. "The chapters me and Lori read were about Reardon. Yeah, that's the name: Michael Reardon," Harper said, pleased. "I went right to the police when I heard about his wife."

The news struck Jake like a blow. "Sylvia Reardon?"

Harper nodded. "That's the one," he said grimly. "Killed just like Lori. I told the police I'd read about Michael in the chapters. They didn't seem to care."

Or they already knew that Reardon had turned up on Drummond's pages, Jake thought. "What'd you do with those chapters?" Jake asked. "Do you still have them?"

Harper shook his head. "Stolen," he said somberly. "The night Lori was killed. Everything was gone. The apartment was torn apart." Harper shook his head again, slower this time. "I told Lori that this kind of business was no place for us, but she wouldn't pay me no mind. She was part of something, you understand. She'd gone back to school wondering if she could manage. When she found she could, she wound up part of some research project. Not reading about it, but making it happen. It was hers." A sadness crept over Harper's features as if he'd just learned he'd lost his Lori. "It got her killed, didn't it? That book got her killed."

"It may have," Jake admitted.

"May have, hell," Harper said, a knowing look settling in his watery eyes. "I know it did. That book and those Harvard types with their big ideas. You can have the whole damn lot," Harper said, a big hand moving to cover his eyes. "Damn 'em all. Damn 'em!"

Jake hated being around crying men, so he removed himself. Back in his Saab, he put a call into information asking for the number of Michael Reardon. The operator reported an unlisted number. Jake thanked her, then called Tommy Dane at home. Jake wondered if Tommy would now answer a few questions he had about the rape and strangulation of Sylvia Reardon.

The phone rang eight times before the baby-sitter answered. The Danes were out for the evening. Any message?

Jake left his name, nothing else.

He drove home looking forward to a few hours' sleep.

Chapter 15

It was still dark when Jake awoke. He was not a morning person, but meeting a man who begins his day rowing his shell on the Charles was not normal either.

Jake swung his legs over the edge of the pullout couch, nearly stepping on the sleeping Watson. Jake stood, then padded quietly to the bathroom. He was trying not to wake Vicki, who was sleeping in Jake's bedroom.

Jake knew full well that if Gloria hadn't come into his life, he would have tried his best to be in bed with Vicki. Even at this hour it was an interesting thought, but only a thought.

Jake took a long, hot shower, dressed, then made the pullout back into a couch. Watson waited at the door, an expectant gleam in his eyes.

A clean fall chill filled the morning air as a pale grayish light signaled the imminent sunrise. Watson's breath hung in the air as he and Jake walked through the nearly empty Harvard Square. The only activity was at the two newsstands and at the entrance to the subway as people scurried for their rides.

Jake headed down JFK Street past Harvard's Kennedy School of Government. Across from the Kennedy School stood clapboard row houses filled with tiny storefront businesses. The Weld Boathouse was across Memorial Drive on the north bank of the Charles River.

Early every morning before the sun heats the city, bringing strong winds with it, and late in the afternoon when the winds die, crews of eights, fours, and doubles row the flat waters of the Charles River.

According to Vicki Shaw, Ellison Kitter started each day rowing his single out of the Weld Boathouse.

Jake opened the massive front door and stepped in behind Watson. The boathouse was essentially a large storage depot for boats, oars, and related paraphernalia. Since the competitive rowing season had ended earlier in October, most of the shells were resting in racks waiting for winter repairs.

Jake stepped around the racks and down the wooden ramp that angled to the river. A white shell broke the plane of the smooth water from under the Larz Anderson Bridge. The stroke was powerful, the pull of the arms hard and even, as was the push of the legs.

"There he is," the boathouse attendant said. "That's Professor Kitter."

"Thanks," Jake said as Watson poked his nose in the murky water. He bared his teeth and retrieved some smelly dead treat. He dropped it on the ground, settled down beside it, and clamped it in his paws just as a boat docked beside him.

An older man—Jake guessed early sixties—with the lanky strength of a swimmer shipped oars and stepped out of the shell. In one fluid motion, he lifted the boat from the water and carried it toward a rack inside. Jake watched with admiration, then followed him in with the pair of ash oars.

"Professor Kitter?"

The man turned to Jake with a look of caution. "Yes? I'm Ellison Kitter."

Jake set the oars across two sawhorses. "I'm Jake Eaton, a private investigator," he said as the professor took a towel from a gym bag and wiped the sweat from his glistening bald head. "I'd like to speak with you, if you have a minute."

"Me?" Kitter worked on a questioning grin. "What on earth for?" he asked, again digging into the bag, this time pulling out a fleece vest. He slid it on and zipped it up.

"I was hoping you could fill in some blanks regarding Bruce Drummond," Jake said. "Vicki Shaw told me that you were working with him."

"We spoke," the professor corrected. "I would hardly call that working together." He studied Jake with mild suspicion. "How is it you know Vicki?" he asked. "She hasn't been around in a while."

"She is now," Jake said. "I'm looking into something for her."

"Oh?" The professor said, stepping aside as another rower carrying a shell made his way down to the water. "Looking into what?" he asked, wiping his arms dry with the towel.

"Bruce Drummond's murder."

The professor stopped wiping. "Bruce Drummond's murder?" he wheezed out. "Is that why you're here? You think I can help you find out who did such a vile thing?"

"It's possible," Jake said, glancing at Watson, who nibbled on his slimy treat. "It would certainly help if I knew what Drummond wanted from you."

"That's simple enough," Kitter said, relaxing a bit. "He wanted information. We spoke perhaps a half dozen times, that was it."

"Spoke about what?"

Kitter dried his legs, then turned to wipe the water from the boat's white fiberglass hull. "He came asking about my specialty: human motivation." The towel stopped momentarily as the professor glanced up at Jake. Kitter declared, "I'm the reigning expert on what makes men do what they do. Bruce was interested in that."

"As it related to?" Jake asked.

Kitter hesitated, looking past Jake as if into some great distance. He cut his eyes back to Jake. "You strike me as a man who seldom asks a question that he doesn't already know the answer to. Why do you think Mr. Drummond sought me out?"

"He wanted information on the DeSalvo case," Jake answered. "He wanted details about a conspiracy."

"Possible conspiracy," the professor corrected, as if Jake were a misspoken student. "Did Vicki provide you with that information?"

"She did."

"Then she probably also told you that it was at her request that I agreed to speak with Bruce Drummond about human motivational factors. It's a field with wide implications," Kitter said, resuming his wiping. "Say you own a factory and are paying workers ten dollars an hour. If you raise their pay to fifteen an hour, should you expect fifty percent more company loyalty and product? You'd be a fool if you did."

"What should I expect?" Jake asked.

"Depends on your objective," Kitter said. "Loyalty might be motivated by one offering, increased productivity by another. Without coming right out and saying it, Drummond was asking a lot of questions relating to loyalty."

Jake stepped out of the professor's way as Kitter moved to the other side of the shell. "Or," Jake asked, "if loyalty could be bought?"

Kitter smiled kindly. "As I said, you ask about what you know. Very consistent, very methodical. I appreciate both. And, yes, loyalty was a topic, as were other motivators."

"Money?" Jake asked, wondering what it would cost to buy a confession to thirteen murders.

"Of course, money." Kitter's expression turned to admiration. "Drummond had developed an interesting concept. Imagine a human pyramid where each successive level is dependent on the strength of those below. Add to it the restriction that the men could look only straight ahead. They never know who stands beside them, below them, or above on their very shoulders. It's a human pyramid built on strength and trust, created by the man standing at the top, the man who would be most vulnerable, has the farthest to fall if the pyramid crumbles."

"Drummond thought such a structure possible?" Jake asked.

"That was his question. Drummond wanted to know if a conspiracy of silence built in such a fashion would be possible."

"And your answer?"

Kitter stopped wiping. "Anything is possible if properly motivated," he said. "I told Drummond that his pyramid would work if—and it is a large if—if each man's need was clearly defined and satisfied."

"Sounds like a job for you, professor," Jake said. "Is that the sort of thing a man with your expertise could formulate?"

"Meaning, could I do it? Yes, I could. So could others."

"Neil Ebberhardt, for instance?"

Kitter straightened up slowly, the friendliness gone from his face. "Why do you ask about Dr. Ebberhardt?" he asked coolly.

Jake shrugged. "I don't know. Vicki said you and he began your careers in the same field. I just thought—"

"We *were* in the same academic discipline," the professor corrected him, his tone underscoring the past tense. "I have moved on. Neil is where Neil is. I couldn't care less about a man who has his name on a building." Kitter paused, his expression making it plain that any further questions about Ebberhardt would end their conversation. "Anything else?" he asked crisply.

Jake filed the emotional reaction and continued. "The pyramid you just described," he said. "If someone were writing a book exposing this hypothetical conspiracy of silence—"

"That would not be tolerated. It would have to be prevented, of course."

"Even if it meant killing those who were writing it?" Jake asked.

Kitter sighed. "Survival is the strongest motivator we have, Mr. Eaton. I warned Vicki that if her theory about DeSalvo not being the Strangler were correct, she and Drummond both could be in danger."

"Then why didn't you stop her?" Jake asked incredulously.

"Because I didn't believe there was any factual basis to the theory," the professor said. "You must remember, I know Vicki. I know her well. Neil Ebberhardt had wounded her pride when he limited her institute access. She wanted to lash out at Neil for the way he had treated her. Locking her out of the institute, casting aspersions on her research abilities . . . it was terrible the way Neil behaved. I saw Vicki's association with Bruce Drummond as a way of getting back at Neil. I didn't think there was more to it than that."

"Then why spend time with Drummond?" Jake asked.

Kitter shook his head, not following. "I told you, Vicki asked me to."

"That might explain the first meeting," Jake said, "but why all the others? Why waste your valuable time if you thought there was no factual basis for Drummond's theory? What motivated you, professor?"

Kitter looked defiant. "I don't know what you're getting at, but I don't like your tone, young man."

"Oh, I think you do," Jake said. "It's pretty obvious you don't like Neil Ebberhardt. I don't know why, but maybe you wanted to get back at Neil as much as Vicki did."

"Preposterous!"

"Not preposterous if you're telling the truth," Jake pressed. "You said you didn't think Vicki was in danger because there was no factual basis for her belief that DeSalvo was innocent."

"That is correct," Kitter said stiffly.

"Yet you met six times with Drummond, feeding his growing conspiracy theory. You were adding fuel to the fire, professor."

"I resent that!"

"Vicki carried a spear, ready to chuck it at Neil Ebberhardt," Jake continued. "You sharpened it by talking to Bruce Drummond, hoping for the greatest pain when Vicki hurled it and it struck your old foe."

The professor threw down the towel. "You don't know what you're talking about," he snapped. "I answered Drummond's questions as a favor to Miss Shaw. I will not answer any more of yours! Now, if you'll excuse me." Kitter picked up his bag, then spun on his heel. He glared at Watson, then quickly back at Jake. "Kindly remove yourself and your dog from the premises," he said, storming off. "Right this minute!"

Watson looked up at the noise, but the smelly edible commanded his attention.

Chapter 16

Jan Rybicki stared at the powerful hands that held the knife, then at the big man's eyes as they slithered down her body. She tried slamming the door, but his foot blocked it. He stepped inside and tossed down the briefcase. The door closed behind him.

"What do you want?" she asked, her pulse pounding in her throat.

Scott had left her apartment minutes ago. He often regretted leaving, buzzed the intercom, and came back. Jan enjoyed the sexy game. Sometimes—like now—when she opened the door for Scott's return, she wore nothing but a smile and a towel.

Jan felt poised over an abyss, still she notched up her courage. "My boyfriend's in the back room," she threatened. "Leave before he sees you. If you go, I won't say anything. I promise."

"I saw him get in his car," the big man said, an intimacy in his voice. "We're alone, Vicki."

Her roommate's name nearly buckled Jan's knees. "Vicki?" she said, swaying. "I'm not Vicki, I'm—"

"Shut up."

The evenly spoken words chilled her. Jan stepped backward to escape, but the intruder's free hand reached out and grabbed her by the arm.

"We missed you at the party," he said. "After I went to all that trouble to round up some puppies, you didn't even show up. How do you think I felt about that?"

Jan looked up at him beseechingly. His eyes were dilated, the pupils dark, wide pools. He tightened his grip. "I had to come find you. Watch you," he said.

"You're hurting me!" Jan cried out.

The big man didn't care. He smiled vaguely. Her pain didn't concern him. What did concern him was the manuscript. He jerked his gaze restlessly around the room until he saw the papers on the desk. He moved toward them, pulling Jan in his wake. He forced her into a chair, the knife point inches from her throat.

"Is this all of it?" he asked with a nod toward the papers. "I want everything." Suddenly he sounded rushed, angry. "Your man Drummond said you had the rest."

He leaned over Jan, his face close to hers as if about to offer some sensible advice. "He asked that you forgive him," the man said, strangely exuberant. "He was pleading for his life over the sounds of the dogs. He was crying, really. Begging. I may have said I would spare him. I may not have. The point is, Drummond thought I said I would. It was something for him to believe in during those last agonizing minutes." He drew the knife along her cheek. "Do you have something to believe in?" he taunted. "An imaginary boyfriend to pop out and save you, maybe?"

She turned sharply to him. She couldn't just give in to the situation. She had to think of something. "There's a private detective on his way here right now."

"Oh, I *am* scared."

"He'll be here any minute. If you leave—"

"Does he have a name?" the big man asked, his concentration more intense.

Jan felt dizzy. She had had the man's card in her hand. He'd *given* it to her. The name? The name? Oh, why hadn't she paid more attention?

The big man relaxed. "I didn't think so."

"Eaton!" Jan gushed. "Jake Eaton. He was here a few days ago looking for the manuscript."

The intruder's head bobbed in the direction of the desk. "Not much of a detective if he couldn't find it," he said, loosening Jan's towel. His eyes brightened at the whiteness of her skin.

"Let me go!"

"That's what Drummond said. Then he told me your address. He said I'd get what I wanted here. Can you imagine what that is, little one?"

Jan covered her breasts, her chest heaving from the quick, short breaths. She clamped her eyes shut. *Make him be gone. Make him be gone. Please, please, when I open my eyes, make him be gone.* She heard the rustling of papers and stole a peek.

The intruder was clearing the desk, stuffing page after page of manuscript into his briefcase. Without thinking of the consequences if she failed, Jan bolted for the door. Both hands fumbled for the knob, turning it, turning it, turning it; her hands trembled, her mind flooded with panic and pain as his fist struck. She lost her balance and fell.

He knelt beside her, his breath warm and moist against her ear. "You brought the Strangler back to life, Miss Shaw. It's only right you should spend some time with him."

"Nnn . . ." She couldn't speak. "I . . . I'm . . . nnn . . . not . . ."

He struck her again to silence her, then went back to collecting the papers.

Jake bought two coffees at the Montrose Spa, one for himself and one for Vicki Shaw. Rosie put the lids on and slid them across the counter.

"Up early, eh, Jake?" she beamed.

"Up early," Jake said with a pleasant nod. "Took Watson for a stroll along the river. Sun wasn't even up."

Carmine turned away from the bagel he was toasting for a customer. "Exercise," he said emphatically. "See what I tell you, Rose? Everybody exercise, even Jake. That's how you lose weight."

Rosie's finger was a waving rod. "Don' talk about diet, Carmine! Don' start." Her beautiful black eyes were slinging darts.

"I'd take her advice, Carmine," Jake said, playing the peacemaker. "Never start a fight with a woman this early in the day."

Jake grabbed the coffees and ducked out the door. Watson trotted contentedly alongside, his tail cranking in small circles. When they crossed Martin Street, Jake's heart sank at the sight of the police car parked in front of his apartment building. He quickened his pace, reaching the walkway into the building just as Lieutenant Dane came back toward the street.

Watson, his body as loose as a slinky, ambled up to the lieutenant. Tommy bent down for a quick pat, his eyes never leaving Jake. "Out early, aren't you, Jake?" Dane asked.

"Very," Jake said, not telling the rest of it.

Dane nodded toward the two coffees. "A little early for company," he said.

"Gloria stayed over," Jake lied. "I'd invite you in, but you know how it is."

"Yeah, I know how it is." The lieutenant took a cigarette from his pack and lit it as two red-faced joggers chugged by. He watched them round the corner onto Avon Street, then he turned back to Jake, the figure of a troubled man. "Got your message," he said.

"Oh, that," Jake said. "I'd almost forgotten I left one."

"You didn't leave one," Dane said. "Nothing more than you called. What was on your mind that hour of the night?"

Jake put the hot cups on the hood of a car, then explained to Tommy about his conversation with James Harper.

"He told me he'd recently done some interesting reading about attorney Michael Reardon," Jake said. "In fact, he told me more in half an hour than you have in a week. The only thing you've given me so far is that Ruth Hill was hot for anything in pants, and we both know that was a lie."

Dane let his eyes wander to the smoke rising from his cigarette. "No more lies, Jake," he said eventually. "Here's a tip about that kennel where you found Drummond's body."

"I'm listening."

"It was once the training facility for Boston PD's canine division," Dane said. "Every police dog was trained there before the place was shut down years back."

Jake had asked Vicki Shaw why she didn't go to the police for help. Her response was that Drummond had thought the police were involved. Now, here was Dane talking about a closed training facility used to murder his friend. Who but someone with connections to Boston PD would have known about such a place?

The question rattled Jake, but he said nothing. Instead, he kept his eyes locked onto Dane, whose chin jutted out as if his tie were too tight. But it wasn't the tie causing the discomfort. It was Dane's sense of loyalty. Dane bled police force blue. To say something against one of his own in the department was a struggle. Dane was struggling and Jake knew why: Dane too thought that cops were involved.

"Drummond came to see me a few weeks ago about a retired cop named Curtis Nash," Dane added.

"Let me guess," Jake said. "Nash worked canine patrol."

Dane shook his head. "I wish it was that simple," he said. "Internal Affairs gave me Nash's name when I began my investigation weeks ago."

"Hold it a second," Jake said. "You had already investigated someone Drummond was just checking into?"

Dane shook his head. "I didn't say that. I said I had a name. I said Drummond came looking for information."

"Did you give him any?"

Again Dane shook his head. "I did not," he said matter-of-factly.

When Jake asked for an explanation, Dane told him how word of the Drummond-Shaw manuscript sent angry waves through Boston PD. Homicide Division in particular had no faith that Drummond would look for the truth, let alone tell it if ever found. The obvious happened; cops closed ranks. Drummond couldn't get the time of day from anyone in uniform, including Tommy Dane.

Fighter that he was, Drummond raised hell. He notified the then attorney general in the case, now Senator Conrad Fowler, and told him he needed leverage to open a few mouths. Fowler looked over the situation and stepped in with a fresh view. He said to take the renewed interest in the case that the Drummond-Shaw manuscript was creating and consider it an opportunity to prove once and for all that the rumors surrounding the investigation are only that: rumors.

"Fowler wanted a new internal investigation?" Jake asked. "A United States senator?"

Dane nodded. "He did. Not enthusiastically at first, but eventually he was all for it."

"What made him change his mind?" Jake asked.

Dane shrugged. "I don't know," he said. "Even when the worst news started coming in, Fowler never blinked."

"What news was that?"

Dane took another drag on his cigarette. "The women—Churchwell, Reardon, and Hill—weren't just raped and strangled, Jake. Whoever killed them left them in the identical poses of the Strangler's original victims. All were found in bed naked, legs spread apart. Around their necks tied with ferocious strength was a bow."

"Original poses?" Jake could hardly believe what he'd just repeated.

Dane flipped the last of his cigarette into the street. "That's why we clamped down on the news reports, Jake. We didn't want the city to panic. Homicide was reeling over this."

"What about Senator Fowler?" Jake asked.

"What do you mean?"

"The Strangler was his investigation. Now women start turning up in identical poses. The thought must have crossed Fowler's mind that maybe DeSalvo *wasn't* really the Boston Strangler," Jake said. "Did he once ask that your internal investigation slow down or stop?"

"No reason to," Dane said as if he'd anticipated Jake's question. "I'm back on the street chasing leads again, Jake. My internal investigation is being put on hold for a bit."

"I don't follow."

"Commander Hoenig," Dane said, pulling another cigarette from the pack. "He wants every man on the street—including me."

"Hunting for the Strangler he should have arrested thirty years ago?" Jake quipped.

Dane shook his head. "Hunting for a copycat," he said, lighting up.

"A copycat?" Jake asked disbelievingly.

"That's the official word. It'll be all over the news by tonight. Hoenig's making an official announcement at noon," Dane said, removing an envelope from his pocket and handing it to Jake. "Take this. I stopped by to make sure you got it."

"What is it?"

"A little something on Curtis Nash. Until I'm back in business with Internal Affairs, it's of no use to me. Consider it a peace offering for that little lie I told you about Ruth Hill's past," Dane said, turning toward his car. He opened the door. "Say hello to Gloria for me." He got in, started the engine, and drove off.

Vicki was washing her face in the bathroom when Jake and Watson entered the apartment. Jake put the two coffees in the microwave to reheat them, his thoughts spinning around the possibility that a copycat was on the loose. The thought gave him an instant headache.

Vicki, dressed in jeans and an extra large Harvard sweatshirt that stopped at her knees, came into the kitchen with quick, light steps.

"I saw you out the window," she said anxiously. "You came along right after that man rang the buzzer."

Jake explained who the man was.

"And you were standing there with two coffees?" Her voice rose an octave.

Jake filled Vicki in on Gloria. "Tommy knows she stays here occasionally. I told him I was just delivering her morning cup," he said, then told Vicki he'd be gone for a while.

"Where?"

"To see a retired cop."

Chapter 17

Curtis Nash was working in his garden on a strip of land sandwiched between the Charles River and Soldiers Field Road. The city had allocated dozens of community garden plots for citizens who had a passion for growing things but had no land. All you had to do was get on a waiting list and hope that your name got called. Curtis Nash's name had been called years ago. According to his wife, Curtis spent part of each day tending his ten-by-twenty rectangle of earth.

Jake parked in the lot and walked along the river until he came upon a roundish man bent over a rake. He was in his mid-sixties and had a fat belly. A portable radio sat atop a nearby plastic cooler. A caller on the talk show said the Red Sox ought to fire their manager.

The man stopped working the soil when he noticed Jake's shadow on the ground before him. He straightened up with difficulty, his right hand rubbing his lower back.

"Curtis Nash?" Jake asked. "Your wife said I'd find you here."

"So?" He was leaning on the rake.

Jake motioned toward the man's garden. Plants killed by frost were piled neatly in one corner. The earth was raked flat, white bonemeal sprinkled on top like powdered sugar. "Not much of a gardener myself," Jake admitted, "but I've always heard that preparing the soil is half the battle."

"Battle, hell. It's where you win the war," the man said. "I'm Nash. What can I do for you?"

"I'd like to ask you a few questions."

"Something tells me it's not about gardening," Nash said suspiciously.

"No," Jake admitted. "Your name has been associated with a friend of mine."

"And who might that friend be?" Nash questioned.

"Bruce Drummond," Jake tossed out, but Nash didn't swing.

"Never heard of him," he said. "Should I have?"

"Perhaps not," Jake said, trying another tack. "It could be that someone working for him contacted you: Lori Churchwell." Nash said nothing, his eyes fixed steadily on Jake. "Did you speak with her?"

The question made Nash shift uncomfortably on his feet. "I may have," he said, working out some strategy. "Now that I think of it, yeah. She called. I told her she had the wrong number."

But Jake didn't have the wrong man. The envelope that Dane had given him explained in detail Officer Curtis Nash's career with Boston PD. It was an undistinguished career except for the fact that throughout his fifteen years on the force, Nash had tried to early-out with every conceivable medical claim. In short, the guy was a goldbrick.

His career began when he got out of the police academy. Nash then spent ten years in squad cars before being assigned to canvas neighborhoods with a composite pencil sketch of what the Boston Strangler might have looked like. The drawing was so vague, it could have been the likeness of anyone. Still, Nash failed to generate any leads.

A year after DeSalvo went to prison as the confessed Strangler, Curtis Nash retired from the force on a disability pension. His early-out was the result of a nervous breakdown suffered after his partner—Doug Turner—pulled his service revolver and fired at an unarmed man caught stealing a car.

"Lori Churchwell was calling people who had something to do with the Boston Strangler case," Jake said. "You did work it?"

"Me and a hundred other guys," Nash snorted. "Besides, that's ancient history. I don't think about it anymore," he said, putting his rake back to work.

"What about your partner?" Jake asked, feeling at once that he'd hit an unsuspected nerve. "Do you ever think about him?"

Nash cut Jake a look. "*Former* partner," he corrected. "Fact is, I wouldn't piss on Doug Turner if he were on fire right here at my feet. I got no use for guys like that." Nash pounded the rake hard against the ground. "No use."

Jake asked why.

"Because," Nash said, straightening, "Doug stepped off the deep end while riding with me. I had four other partners in my career, and none ever got out of line. I was a clean cop. They knew if they spit on the sidewalk, my foot would be on their pants before it dried. Doug knew that too, but he didn't seem to care." Nash's brow creased. "The hardest thing I ever had to do was take the stand and testify against one of my own kind," he said.

Jake kicked at a stone with the toe of his shoe. "Are you talking about the shooting?" he asked.

"I am."

"What happened?"

"Doug went ballistic," Nash said. He explained that he and Doug were following a suspect in a stolen car down Columbus Avenue in Boston's South End. They pulled the suspect over. Doug went around to the driver's side. Nash stayed back to radio in the plate number. Before the plate had cleared, Nash heard shots.

"Doug had his service revolver out, firing at the suspect," Nash said. "He'd gotten off three rounds before I got to him and made him stop. Lucky the driver ducked, or Doug would have gone up for murder one."

"Did Turner say why he fired?" Jake asked.

"Sure. He said the driver pulled a gun of his own. But no gun was ever found in the car or near it. I didn't have any choice but to testify against him," Nash admitted.

"Must've been tough on you," Jake said, knowing the eleventh commandment that cops live by: protect your own. It was a directive that went beyond allegiance to a uniform or a badge. Protect your own meant risking your life on the streets. It also meant taking the witness stand and telling less than the truth when a fellow officer's neck was in the noose. Jake knew of more than one occasion when needed evidence was suddenly found where before no evidence existed. He also knew of weapons that appeared out of nowhere when an officer's claim was self-defense. It didn't happen often, but it happened. The reason? Crooks don't play by the rules; why should the cops?

"Damn right it was tough," Nash said bitterly. "Guilty or not, it ruined me. Guys I'd known for years wouldn't sit down for a beer. After a while, I couldn't bear to go to work. When I forced myself to go, I couldn't get anything done. Pretty soon, a doctor recommended I hang it up for my health." Nash offered a weak smile. "Here I am," he said.

"What happened to Turner?" Jake asked.

"He died a few years ago. I don't know the details."

"Did he work the Strangler case with you?" Jake wondered.

The question seemed to take Nash by surprise. "No, no. You got the timing all wrong," he protested. "DeSalvo was arrested in 1964. Doug was assigned to be my partner in 1972. I explained all this to that Churchwell lady. I said she was all wet thinking that Doug had anything to do with DeSalvo."

Interesting, Jake thought. He asked if the purpose of Churchwell's call was to get information about Doug Turner.

"That's right," Nash said.

"Why didn't she call Doug Turner herself?" Jake asked.

"I told you, Doug's dead," Nash said without feeling. "Besides, every cop knows that Churchwell and Drummond weren't looking for the truth. They had their own damn agenda, so I hung up." His arm swept down. "Bang!" he said, a nasty smile curling on his face.

"I thought you never heard of Bruce Drummond," Jake said, wiping away Nash's smile.

Nash glared. "Is that all?" he said, wanting it to be. "I'm here to work my garden."

"One more question," Jake said. "Did Doug Turner have anything to do with the canine division?"

Nash looked surprised at the question. "Dogs? No way. Doug wasn't on the force long enough to go with canine."

"Oh? How long was that?" Jake asked.

"A few months, maybe."

"A few months and he was standing trial?" Jake said. "If he was that shaky, how'd he ever get out of the academy?"

Nash bent to his rake. If he knew the answer, he wasn't telling. Jake walked back to his car, thinking that this garden was producing nothing.

Chapter 18

The October sun warmed Jake's face as he shifted into second gear on the highway that parallels the Charles River. He was on his way back to his apartment when the cellular phone rang. "Yes?" he said into the receiver.

"You don't sound too happy," the voice said.

"I'm not."

"This will make you feel worse," the voice added as Jake finally recognized who was on the other end.

"Frank Cowen? What the hell are you up to?"

"I'm up to my neck in dead women," Frank said gloomily, then gave Jake the address.

Jake put down the phone and gunned the Saab toward Central Square. A cold chill settled over him when he saw the police cars blocking the street. He jerked to a stop in the only space available— in front of a fire hydrant. He threw open the door and jumped out.

Patrolman Stewart Chan directed traffic around the ambulance, his short, fat arms swinging like the blades of a windmill. "You can't park there, Jake," Stewart told him. "I'll have to write you up."

Jake paid no attention to anything except the knot in his stomach. As he ran to the front porch of Vicki and Jan's building, two paramedics blocked the hall with a collapsible metal gurney. With difficulty, they angled it around the first landing, then headed up the stairs. Jake squeezed by them, taking the stairs two at a time. He stopped in the hall until forensics finished dusting the doorjamb, then he entered the living room. Sergeant Frank Cowen was sketching the crime scene, noting the position of the overturned chair and the broken lamp. Frank looked up from his sketch, frowning. "Didn't take you long," he said, an edge in his tired voice. A camera flashed at the far end of the hall. Frank gestured with his pad. "She's in the bedroom. Have a look if you want."

Jake stepped into the hall, then moved steadily toward the photographer near Jan Rybicki's bed. Another flash silhouetted the forensics expert marking and bagging evidence.

Jake took one look at Jan Rybicki's naked body propped up on pillows at the head of the bed, then turned his gaze to the female forensics expert. She was wearing dark blue stirrup pants and a gray top. Jake hated stirrup pants. He hated the way they looked, the way they stretched, the way they bagged at the knees and drooped at the rear. He jammed his mind full of all the things he hated about stirrup pants but still felt the cold, vacant eyes of Jan Rybicki staring at him.

He wanted to reach past the red bow tied around her delicate neck and close the eyes. He wanted to pull the rumpled sheet over her spread legs and exposed sex. He wanted five minutes alone with the animal who robbed the life from this once vibrant young woman.

Jake lowered his head and turned back to the living room. He stood at the desk, now stripped clean, remembering the piles of papers he'd seen here only days before. He looked through a partially opened drawer. Empty.

"Has Boston been here?" Jake asked.

"No, and Boston won't be," Frank said with finality. "Hoenig's thrown in the towel." Frank beamed as if he'd personally kicked the commander back across the river. "We're in the hunt on this one, Jake. We'll be working Ruth Hill, too."

"Who's running the investigations?" Jake asked.

"Lieutenant Stellar, Cambridge PD. He's tough as nails, Jake. A real bare knuckler," Frank said with pride.

Jake knew Stellar's mercurial reputation. He survived by being the best investigator Cambridge had ever had, backing it up with a heavy caseload and an even higher arrest percentage.

Jake glanced back at the bare desk. "Did Stellar take anything from this desk when he left? Some papers, maybe?" Jake asked.

Frank shook his large head. "Wasn't anything to take. Stellar figures that after the perp raped and strangled Rybicki, he took what he wanted. Why?"

"No reason."

Frank came closer. "You wouldn't be holding anything back, would you, Jake?" he asked suspiciously. "I leveled with you earlier about Ruth Hill. I'd like to think you'd do the same with me," he said as the paramedics entered the room. Cowen told them to wait, because the medical examiner was on his way.

"Who found the body?" Jake asked.

"An airline attendant," Frank answered. "Seems the victim didn't make it to Logan for a flight out. The victim has a roommate," Frank said, flipping back through his pad until he found the name. "Vicki Shaw. We haven't located her yet. Neighbors downstairs said she was a grad student and that she's been gone for a few days."

"I'm sure you'll find her," Jake said at the door.

"Oh, we'll find her, just like we're going to find the killer. We'll show Boston PD how it's done. Count on it," Frank bragged as the medical examiner—puffing hard from the three flights of stairs—entered. When Sergeant Cowen took him to the body, Jake left.

Outside, the street had filled with television crews setting up to broadcast live remotes. On the sidewalks, the curious had gathered for a firsthand look at bad news being made.

One of the reporters, a tiny Asian woman with shiny black hair and a bright smile made for the small screen, had cornered Lieutenant Roy Stellar.

Stellar had a black beard, cut close to his olive skin. He towered over the young reporter, alertly taking in the activity around him. He stood woodenly, his back straight as a plank waiting for the reporter's lead-in to begin. At last, the cameraman's countdown reached two, then one, then the cue to start.

Jake got closer to listen as the reporter looked somberly into the camera. "The murder of a second woman in this normally quiet neighborhood near Harvard University has shattered the calm. Six days ago, the body of Ruth Hill—a university employee—was

discovered on Cambridge Common. She had been raped and strangled. This morning, the body of a twenty-six-year-old woman, whose
name has not been released, was found in this top-floor apartment.
Preliminary reports indicate she too had been raped and strangled.
To shed some light on these two gruesome murders, we are joined
by the man in charge of this investigation, Lieutenant Roy Stellar,
Cambridge police. Thank you for being with us."

Stellar forced a smile.

"What can you tell us about the similarities between these two
crimes?" she asked.

"I can't answer that right now," Stellar said. "Cambridge police is
just beginning our investigation."

"Which is a story in and of itself," the young reporter said eagerly
into the lens. "Isn't it true that Boston Homicide has been in charge?
And that they haven't wanted any outside help?"

Stellar nodded stiffly. "That's all behind us," he said diplomatically.
"As of last night, we are joining forces, working together every step
of the way."

"Then the latest murder had nothing to do with Commander
Hoenig's decision to let Cambridge work the case?" the reporter
asked.

"None," Stellar said. "The commander decided to lift the news
blockade and to seek our help long before the present victim was
discovered."

"When was that?"

"Approximately seven this morning."

"Then you and Boston PD are no longer fighting over case jurisdiction?" the reporter pressed.

Stellar had been around too long and was too smart to run with
that offering. He answered that a turf war had never been a problem. It must have been something the press made up to fill its pages.

"We will continue our positive working relationship with Boston,"
he said. "The press will be given necessary briefings until the man
responsible for these terrible crimes is off the streets and behind
bars. There is no jurisdictional wrangling when it comes to that."

The reporter beamed. "The public will appreciate that, Lieutenant. You could begin those briefings by letting our audience know

if there is any connection between Miss Hill and the woman found dead today. Did they know each other?" the reporter asked.

"They may have," Stellar replied. "Miss Hill worked for the roommate of the deceased." Stellar glanced at his notes. "Her name is Shaw. Vicki Shaw. There is some speculation that the killer may have mistaken his target. We're looking into that possibility." Stellar started to leave, but another question called him back.

"Before you go, Lieutenant," the reporter began. "There are rumors in Boston that Sylvia Reardon was also a strangler victim."

"I'd prefer not to comment on that," Stellar said firmly, but the young reporter would not give up.

"And, that this strangler is copying the brutal style of the infamous Albert DeSalvo."

"That is the theory we are now operating under," Stellar said. "Boston has been most cooperative in providing leads. I think I should state here that the people of Boston and Cambridge have no reason to panic. We expect to make an arrest soon. Now, if you'll excuse me."

When the lieutenant turned away, the reporter stared back to the camera. "You heard it here," she said, adding drama. "A copycat killer is on the prowl, but an arrest is hoped for soon. This is Melissa Woo reporting."

Arrests are always hoped for, Jake thought as something else stuck in his memory. He'd warned Jan Rybicki about intruders, about casually letting people into her apartment. He wished like hell she'd heeded it.

Jake hurried back to his car, certain that the killer had made his first attempt on Vicki. He fired the engine, then before driving off had second thoughts. He picked up his phone and put in a call to Gloria at her new house. When she answered, Jake suggested a plan—a plan that would provide Vicki with a safer place to stay.

As usual, Gloria was happy to help.

Chapter 19

Vicki Shaw stood in a sad trance, her feelings spinning on an emotional rotisserie. "I don't believe you," she snapped, glaring at Jake as he pulled down two wool sweaters from the top of the hall closet. "Jan . . . Jan is . . ." She cut her eyes away toward the ceiling. A tear appeared on her cheek. "Jan can't be dead. She can't be!"

"It was meant to be you," Jake told her. "That's the only way it makes sense."

Vicki wrapped her arms across her chest. "Me?"

Jake continued to pack, staying out of the way of Vicki's torment. He looked around for his down vest. He put it in the bag, then set the bag by the door.

Vicki's hands wandered to her throat. "I don't want to do this anymore," she said, peering strangely at Jake. "I *can't!*"

"Afraid you don't have any choice," Jake said, stuffing another bag with clothes. "Neither of us does."

"What do you mean by that?" she asked faintly.

"I mean things have changed, Vicki," Jake said in an even, sober voice. "Word of a strangler will lead the news tonight, scaring the hell out of everyone but, more importantly, tipping off the killer that he murdered the wrong woman. It won't take him long to look for you here."

"But how would he know?"

"He'll know of my connection to Drummond. If he doesn't, he'll find out soon enough and pay us a visit. Only," Jake said steadily,

106

"we won't be here." He set the other bag by the door. "Where's your computer?"

"On the desk."

"Get it," Jake said, glancing quickly around the apartment. "There's a printer where we're going. I think it's time I had a look at your manuscript." He tossed Vicki a hooded sweatshirt. "Put that on, hood up. I don't want to take a chance of anyone spotting you. Go down the back stairs to the rear entrance and across the yard between the two buildings. I'll have the car waiting."

Vicki took the dark blue shirt. With one sleeve, she wiped away her tears.

Jake drove toward Boston Harbor and *Gamecock* in an adrenaline buzz. Gloria and Jake had planned on one more short cruise up the coast before the cold weather set in. During his call to Gloria earlier, Jake asked if she'd like to get started this afternoon. Nothing special. A sail north, maybe. Just the two of them, plus crew.

Crew? Since when do we need crew? Gloria had wanted to know. After she nixed the idea, she asked Jake what he really had in mind, and he told her the simple truth.

"I want to keep Vicki Shaw alive," he said.

Vicki sat in the passenger seat, the hood covering most of her face. Jake leaned forward for a look. He wanted to make sure she was really in there.

"How're you holding up?" he asked. Her silence was answer enough.

Jake checked the rearview mirror for any signs he was being followed. Other than Watson's serious face, he saw nothing out of the ordinary. "Mind if I ask you a few questions?" he said.

More silence.

Jake forged ahead. "You said earlier that Drummond had a few names he wanted Lori Churchwell to—"

"Do we have to talk about this now?" Vicki protested.

"Your pain's not going to go away, Vicki. If we wait for that, we'll wait forever." Jake turned onto Storrow Drive and headed east toward Boston. "Was Curtis Nash one of those names?" He eased into the traffic. "Curtis Nash, Vicki. Does that name mean anything to you?"

The hood moved from side to side.

It was a start, Jake thought. He asked about Doug Turner. "He was a—"

"I know, a cop who got in trouble."

"How do you know that?" Jake asked.

The hood turned, exposing Vicki's face. "Bruce asked about him," she said, her voice distant. "He wanted me to run a check on him the next time I was at the Ebberhardt."

Jake waited expectantly. "And?" he asked.

Vicki shrugged. "It never happened," she said. "'Next time turned out to be the day Professor Ebberhardt locked me out of the files. I never had the chance to look up anything. I'd never seen Bruce so disappointed." Vicki looked around. "Where are we going?"

"You'll see," Jake said. "Did Drummond ever tell you why Turner was important?"

"Not really. In his usual way, he just said he wanted to know everything about Turner there was to know," she said, the memory seeming to shed some light. "But it was at about the same time that Bruce asked me to introduce him to Ellison Kitter," Vicki added.

Kitter? Jake wondered as he drove under the Southeast Expressway and turned toward the marina. "Did Drummond think that the professor knew something of Doug Turner?"

"Yes. Yes, he did."

"What?" Jake asked.

"I don't know," Vicki answered. "Bruce never told me."

"Maybe he didn't tell you, but Drummond always kept notes. It was the reporter in him. Could his notes be on your computer?" Jake asked.

"They might be. We shared diskettes and copied each other's files. Bruce sometimes included notes on his manuscript diskettes. We'll have to search my computer files to find out."

Gladly, Jake thought, tossing out a wild idea. "Do you think Professor Kitter could have been involved in the conspiracy to frame Albert DeSalvo?"

The very idea outraged Vicki. "Of course not! Ellison has one of the most respected minds in the country. Why would he? Besides,"

Vicki added, "I know him as a friend. He wouldn't harm anyone, not Ellison."

Jake slowed for traffic, inching along the narrow streets of Boston's North End. "But a conspiracy would need a brilliant mind to plan some of the details," Jake said. "Plus, I'm talking about the Ellison Kitter of thirty years ago, not the man you know now."

Vicki's head shook in a quick burst. "No. He would never get involved. I know it."

Jake let it slide. He had other questions, and little time before his destination. "You knew Lori Churchwell and Ruth Hill pretty well, didn't you?" he asked.

"Yes."

"How well did you know Sylvia Reardon?"

"I didn't know her at all," Vicki said. "That is, I'd never spoken to her. Bruce interviewed Sylvia and her husband, Michael. From that interview, Bruce drafted some early chapters."

Jake cut her a questioning look. "You had no input in those?"

"None," Vicki said.

"Why not?"

"I couldn't completely abandon my dissertation. Some weeks, I had to work on it. If I didn't continue to show some progress, we would have lost the help of Ruth Hill."

"Meaning the department would have assigned her to someone else?"

"That's right," Vicki said as if she'd wished that very thing had happened. "All I know about the Reardons is that Bruce suspected Michael's involvement in the conspiracy. I know *those* chapters are in the computer. Bruce loaded them so I could print them out for Lori."

"I want to see them," Jake said, glancing at his watch. It was just past one in the afternoon of a sunny October day. He pulled into the Commercial Wharf parking lot and shut off the engine. *Gamecock* lay at the ready, her big diesel engine pushing water out the exhaust tube, her sail covers removed.

"Ever been on a boat before, Vicki?" he asked.

"A boat?" The word seemed to catch in her throat.

"Just do what the captain says," Jake explained, opening the door for Watson. Jake removed the bags from the back. "She'll take care of you."

"She? You're not coming with us?"

"Depends on what I see in that computer of yours," Jake said. "Now, let's go," he encouraged, waving down at Gloria, who had eagerly agreed to help once she'd heard what Jake really had in mind.

In fact, Gloria had endorsed it. "I think hiding her onboard is a wonderful idea," she'd said, delight in her voice. "Very cunning of you, Jake."

"Then you'll do it?"

"I'll have the boat ready when you are," Gloria had said.

She was true to her word.

Chapter 20

Once Jake got the bags and Watson onboard, and Vicki introduced to Captain Gloria, he immediately helped Vicki set up her laptop. Gloria had a printer secured to the chart table for her own navigational computer, but Vicki's software soon proved incompatible.

"I can't get you a hard copy," she explained to Jake. "Mind reading files on the screen?"

Jake didn't mind at all and sat down to read the opening chapter that Drummond had drafted about Michael Reardon. He had scrolled through about ten pages when Gloria called down from *Gamecock*'s deck saying that she was ready to cast off.

Jake popped his head up the companionway. "I need a few more minutes," he said, explaining he was having a difficult time making sense of Drummond's speculations.

"Translation?" Gloria asked, with Watson at her side.

Jake shrugged. "Half hour, maybe forty-five minutes," he said to Gloria's shaking head.

"Can't give it," she replied. "The tide's already past. I need to get out of here if we're to make any time."

Jake climbed into the cockpit and helped Gloria free the lines. With just the spring line secured on the port side, he hauled in the bumpers and stowed them. He gave Gloria a kiss on the way by.

"You all right?" he asked.

"I'm fine. And don't worry. Your passenger will be too. Watson and I will see to that."

Jake bent down and scruffed Watson's neck. "You stay and make sure she's all right, eh, pup?"

Watson barked, then shook his burly head. Jake jumped down to the dock. When Gloria signaled ready, Jake walked the big boat out of her slip. He coiled the last line, then tossed it on deck. Gloria throttled the sloop forward.

"See you in a few hours," Gloria said, energized by the challenge. Jake nodded. "It would help if you could work something out with that printer. I'm from the old school," he said. "I need paper in my hands, not some lines dancing on a small screen."

"I'm sure Vicki and I can figure out something," Gloria said as Vicki climbed into the cockpit, seemingly lost. "See you in a few," Gloria said reassuringly and drove *Gamecock* steadily out the channel.

Jake offered a mock salute, then dashed to his car. In minutes, he was cruising down Brattle Street past the Longfellow estate— now a museum. He pulled to a stop in front of a revolutionary-period colonial painted dark gray. Long before the new rich discovered Cambridge in the 1980s, these imposing homes were typical of old Cambridge architecture, old families, and old Cambridge money. Now, anyone with a million bucks could live here.

Jake parked in the driveway, got out, and walked across the long lawn toward a man removing screens and putting up wood-framed storm windows. The man was more than six feet five inches tall and looked like he weighed only two hundred pounds. A string bean, Jake said to himself.

Jake guessed the man to be in his late fifties. He had little of his brown hair left, but his beard was still prosperous. The man wore a denim work shirt and matching jeans from L.L. Bean. A leather tool belt containing a hammer, screwdriver, and other metal implements hung over the jeans.

Jake cleared his throat to capture the man's attention. The man— screen in hand—turned easily to Jake, his expression a question.

"I understand that Michael Reardon lives here," Jake said.

"That's right."

"Is he in?"

The man's expression turned from curiosity to a condescending grin. "Who wants to know?" he asked, then listened attentively as Jake introduced himself. When Jake finished, the man leaned the screen against the clapboard-sided house. "I'm Michael Reardon," he said, taking out his screwdriver. "As you can see, I'm rather busy."

"I won't stop you," Jake said. "I'd just like to ask a few questions." Michael resumed his work, diligently removing a stubborn screw set deep in the frame. When the screw was in his hand, he said lazily, "Call my secretary if you want an appointment. I don't do business on Saturdays or on my front lawn. No exceptions for private detectives. Sorry," Reardon said, not looking sorry at all.

"I'm working on a case . . ."

Reardon faced Jake as if looking for the slightest sign of intelligence. "Didn't you hear?" he said stubbornly. "Call my office."

"A case that may have something to do with the death of your wife."

A light seemed to spike in the attorney's eyes. "What business of yours is that?" he demanded.

"It's my business to find out about Ruth Hill," Jake said evenly.

Reardon's eyes narrowed to slits. "I know nothing about any Ruth Hill," he said. "Sylvia's death was a random act. You may try to connect her murder to others, but you would be wasting your time."

"I know the connection, Mr. Reardon," Jake said, letting the idea gather its own strength. "I've read part of the manuscript that Bruce Drummond was writing."

Reardon seemed immediately more interested in the conversation. "Are you saying you have a copy?" he asked.

"I might have," Jake said.

"I'd like to see it," Reardon continued. "I'd like to see what was written about me."

"The man who killed Drummond wanted to see a copy, too."

Reardon bristled. "What are you saying?" he demanded. "If you're suggesting I had anything to do with that reporter's death, you're mistaken."

"I'm not suggesting anything," Jake said. "I'm merely making the observation that several people—people linked in various ways to a certain conspiracy—would like to get their hands on that manuscript. Drummond did connect you, Mr. Reardon. He said you played a part in—"

"I don't want to hear it!"

"A part in a conspiracy to frame Albert DeSalvo."

"A lie to begin with, but even if it was true, am I somehow now a murder suspect?" Reardon checked his growing anger. "Is that the way your mind works? I would like to see what a delusional man writes about me, and I immediately become capable of murder."

"Somebody killed four women."

"One of whom was my wife!" Reardon seethed. "Did I kill her, too? Hire someone to do it? What?"

"You tell me," Jake said evenly.

"I am telling you: get off my property! Now! If you don't, I'll call the authorities and press charges. I mean it."

Jake held his ground. He had a general rule against getting pushed around.

"Fine," Reardon said. "Ron Hoenig will gladly put you in your place. He has this thing about private detectives: he hates them."

"Not all," Jake said. "Just me. But why Hoenig?"

"He's a friend, for one thing. For another, he's handling Sylvia's murder investigation."

"Why not Dane?" Jake asked.

"I don't deal with underlings," Reardon said. "Commander Hoenig is personally in charge. Shall I call him? Or will you leave?"

Jake knew brick walls when he bumped into them. He backed away, turned around, and walked slowly to his Saab. With each step, the image of Commander Ronald Hoenig grew stronger in his memory. It was a bitter memory of a ruthless, secretive man whom Jake first met years ago.

Hoenig was deliberate and thorough, a man made for a position of authority—a quality that police department higher-ups recognized in him immediately. They put Hoenig on the fast track, moving him through the ranks of detective, then lieutenant, then head of the special task force in charge of the Boston Strangler investigation. It was Ronald Hoenig who arrested Albert DeSalvo. But Jake's encounter with Hoenig happened years after the Strangler case.

It was fifteen years ago, but Jake could see it as if it were yesterday. Two punks crashed down on an Eaton Agency stakeout by fatally shooting Jake's brother, Max, and beating Jake so severely that he nearly died. The punks had arrest records for robbery, drugs, and car theft but never anything close to murder. The records changed that night in the section of Boston known as the Fens when they aimed a rifle at Max and repeatedly pulled the trigger.

Jake had run toward the shots and Max's cries for help, but the two punks were waiting for him. Like his brother, Jake never saw the attack coming. When their rifle jammed, one of the punks slammed the butt against Jake's head; the other broke Jake's ribs with his relentless kicks.

By the time Jake was well enough to leave the hospital, the two punks had been arrested. Because it was their first time up for murder one, the DA opted for a lesser charge. He got his conviction; they were paroled in less than eighteen months. The first week back on the streets, the two punks were found shot to death in an alley not far from the Fens. No one was ever charged with the crime, but many thought Jake did the shooting. One man in particular—Ronald Hoenig—was convinced that Jake had done it.

But Hoenig's own career was not free of suspicion either. At least one person—Bruce Drummond—believed that Hoenig was the man behind the conspiracy that let the real Boston Strangler go. Internal reviews of that investigation never substantiated the charges. Still Drummond—on more than one occasion—tried to sell Jake on Hoenig's guilt. Without evidence to support Drummond's accusations, Jake ignored his personal dislike of the commander and never believed that Hoenig had pulled a fast one and gotten away with it.

When Jake got back to his car after talking with Reardon, his questions about Hoenig were stacked up like planes trying to land at Logan Airport on a foggy night. What was Hoenig's real interest in Sylvia Reardon's death? Or was he handling the investigation as payback for a long-overdue debt? But a debt to Michael Reardon? Why? How were the two men connected? Was that connection related to the Strangler? Was Bruce Drummond right about the commander?

Jake started his car. He swung around and headed toward Quincy, Marina Bay, Vicki Shaw, and, he hoped, answers.

Chapter 21

Reading the manuscript alone in his rented room, the big man clicked on the television for company. On the screen, a supposedly exciting contest was taking place between a man and a woman, each trying to guess prices of ordinary items found in grocery stores. The man priced a case of canned peas at twenty-five dollars; he lost. The woman bounced with joy, applauding her good fortune. She—and a lucky guest—were on their way to Disneyland.

The big man switched the channel past stock market reports and a soccer game and stopped at a news broadcast. The news anchor spoke of a press conference held earlier in the day. The big man was about to flick the channel one more time when the image of Hoenig appeared on the screen.

The commander was standing on granite steps in front of Boston police headquarters. He held onto the wooden podium, looking splendid and confident in his dark, pin-striped suit. He looked over the bank of microphones, adjusting one to a proper height. "Before I get to my prepared statement, I would like to comment on the death of Jan Rybicki, who was found raped and strangled early this morning in Cambridge."

The shot switched to file footage of the triple-decker that Jan shared with Vicki Shaw. The big man put down the manuscript. He leaned closer to the set.

"Rybicki?" the big man said under his breath as he struggled with a knot burning in his throat. He jumped to his feet, sweeping the hair back from his face. "Rybicki? Where the hell is Vicki Shaw?" he shouted at the screen, wondering if he had killed the wrong woman.

Impossible.

He'd watched the apartment for days. He'd seen the woman come and go, seen her boyfriend do the same at all hours. The big man had picked the time, the place. He'd planned well, just as he'd planned for Drummond. Watching him, watching him, watching him until that day in the park when Drummond shied from the cluster of playful dogs.

What is this? the big man wondered. Is the man who's trying to ruin my family, ruin me, afraid of dogs? He watched more closely until he was certain of the answer, until he was certain how he wanted to use that bit of knowledge. His certainty was the important element. He *knew* beyond a doubt about Drummond's fear. Just as he *knew* beyond any doubt that the woman in the triple-decker was Vicki Shaw.

Now there is this rotten lie on the TV screen. Jan Rybicki? Who the hell cares about Jan Rybicki?

Disgusted, the big man switched off the television, thinking in the quiet. What was it that Drummond had told him as he pleaded for his life? Who was it he should fear?

The big man was not good with names, and that irritated him. He stood at the window looking out at the brick bowfronts across the street. His eyes seemed to focus on a point inside himself as he thought of names. What was it? It was the name that Rybicki had also threatened him with.

He jumped around the alphabet. With each letter, he tried to jar the name to life. He could remember nothing and it infuriated him. "What the hell is that name?" he roared, slamming his fist on the desk and bouncing the phone book on the floor.

He picked up the phone book. Under "Investigators," he started with A and stopped when the name presented itself.

Directly under East Coast Detectives was a listing for The Eaton Agency. He wrote down the address and closed the book.

Five miles south of Boston lies the town of Quincy, Massachusetts, birthplace of two American presidents. It is also home of the well-appointed Marina Bay, where *Gamecock* was tied up.

While Gloria was readying the boat in Commercial Wharf, Jake had instructed her to pass the word that her destination was north to Maine. If Jake and Vicki had been followed, or if anyone came later looking for Jake onboard, information would lead them north, not south to where Gloria actually traveled.

It was just after sunset when Jake stepped onto the Marina Bay docks. He found the familiar blue-hulled sloop tied to a wooden pier at the far end of the marina. Her cabin lights were giving off the glow of a lighted pumpkin.

Jake leaned over the toe rail. Before he could call down, Watson's warning barks rose into the chilly air. Gloria was right behind them, climbing the companionway steps into the cockpit, where she and Jake embraced.

"How'd it go?" Jake asked as the excited Watson scrambled up the stairs for his own hug. Jake obliged.

"The trip went well," Gloria said. "So did the printing. See for yourself."

Inside the cabin, a makeshift workstation complete with humming printer was set up on the chart table. At the dinner table, forward in the main salon, Vicki Shaw—looking comfortable if not content— pored over manuscript pages.

"Come up with anything?" Jake asked, pleased with the printer's progress.

"I'm just going through the latest files that Bruce left with me. I'm not exactly sure what I'm looking for," Vicki admitted as Watson padded by.

"Anything about the ex-cop Doug Turner, Michael Reardon, and Reardon's connection to Ron Hoenig will do for a start," Jake said.

"Your old nemesis?" Gloria asked warily. "What's he got to do with any of this?"

"Good question," Jake admitted. "Michael Reardon brought up his name. Sounded to me like old friends doing each other a favor, but we'll need more than a guess if we're to get anywhere."

Gloria sensed a disquiet in Jake's answer and asked about his visit with Reardon.

"I've now got more questions than answers." Jake turned to Vicki. "Did you print out the Reardon chapters?" he asked.

Vicki held up a small stack of pages. "They're all right here," she said. "Chapters, notes, you name it. Everything Bruce loaded onto my system."

"Come on." Jake motioned Gloria to the settee. "You can help me read through this stuff."

And "stuff" it was: a few pages of the you-are-there approach, some forays into the mind of the Boston Strangler, and some incomplete sketches.

Jake skimmed over what he'd read previously, then on page fifty of the new material he found what he was looking for. He gave Gloria a hopeful wink and began reading intently what Drummond had written.

For some, the arrest of Albert DeSalvo was the end of a two year manhunt. For others, like Michael Reardon, it was the beginning of a criminal conspiracy the likes of which Boston had never experienced.

It is first necessary to understand that Boston is a city of tradition, history, and pride. It is a city of social registers and cotillions. It is a city of enclaves where old money and family names protect with the vigilance of armies. For such families, it is not a city of murder trials and prison sentences, even if one of their own was the Boston Strangler.

Gloria lowered the page, her eyes troubled. "One of their own?" she repeated. "One of whose own?"

Jake turned the page eagerly. "Maybe Drummond will tell us," he said and began to read about Michael Reardon.

According to Drummond, Michael Reardon was a year out of law school and working as a clerk in F. Lee Bailey's firm when Albert DeSalvo went shopping for an attorney. Bailey took the case and the public abuse for so doing. Much of the public wanted to see DeSalvo strung up on Boston Common. After all, the man confessed. Why waste time on a trial? Why relive thirteen gruesome murders? Why not get down to business at the end of a rope?

Bailey feared that a lynching might actually happen. He appealed for help and got it from Massachusetts Attorney General Conrad

Fowler. Fowler was not caught unprepared. He also had concerns regarding Albert's life as well as the safety of his family.

Fowler was ready with a plan when he got the call from Bailey. After all, this was the biggest serial killer case in U.S. history. Boston was in the spotlight. Blunders would ruin careers, and what would be a greater blunder than to have either Albert DeSalvo, his wife, Irmgard, or their two children hurt or killed?

Fowler secured Albert in prison isolation. Then, with F. Lee Bailey's help, Michael Reardon's assignment began: he was to move DeSalvo's wife and children secretly out of state, then at the appropriate time return them to Boston for the trial.

Drummond wrote how Reardon had driven the family to New Hampshire and checked them into a hotel under an assumed name. After a week, he moved them again, this time to a hotel near the Finger Lakes in New York. This process continued week after week, until one night Reardon received a phone call at his home. This time, however, it was not F. Lee Bailey issuing new moving instructions.

According to Drummond, the man never identified himself to Reardon. He simply told Reardon that plans had changed; Albert's wife and children would not be returning to Boston as originally planned. Reardon was to get them to Germany.

This request did not come from F. Lee Bailey, the man on the phone told Reardon. In fact, compliance would result in Reardon's dismissal from Bailey's law firm. Reardon should be ready for, but not fear, such developments. They were for the best.

"Big change," Gloria said.

"DeSalvo's wife was a German national," Jake explained.

"I wasn't talking about that," Gloria said. "I was talking about Reardon."

"I was thinking the same thing," Jake said, and continued reading Drummond's account.

It is the genius of this conspiracy, that Michael Reardon did as he was asked, knowing beforehand that if he did, F. Lee Bailey would treat such insubordination as a kind of treason. So why did Michael Reardon—a man who wanted little else in life other than to practice law with the best—why did he act in such a way as to get fired from one of the top law firms in the country? The answer is simple: Reardon was promised his own practice with his own steady stream of well-paying clients.

After thirty years of practice, the prize of his client list is the world-famous Ebberhardt Institute. What is not widely known is that the Ebberhardt family was one of Reardon's first clients.

The Ebberhardts are one of Boston's finest families. Their name and wealth deflect most . . ."

The chapter ended in midsentence. At the bottom of the page, Drummond had typed: [Check institute files on Walter E.]

"Damn," Jake said, wishing he had one additional page. "Who's Walter E?"

"Walter Ebberhardt," Gloria answered. "Neil's brother."

"Didn't know he had one," Jake admitted. "Why didn't Drummond talk to Walter directly instead of leaving a note to check the files?"

"Because he's not that easy to locate." Vicki said. "I remember Lori mentioning she was having a hard time tracking him down."

"Walter Ebberhardt was one of the people Drum wanted contacted?" Jake asked.

"Yes."

"Now wait a second," Gloria said, attempting a defense. "The Ebberhardts are friends of mine. Drummond can't be trying to blame any of this mess on them!"

"So it would seem," Jake said, aware that the mood inside the boat was tense. He didn't want to provoke Gloria, but he was thinking that he should have a look at the file on Walter E. himself. "I think someone should fix us dinner, even if it has to be me," he said to break the mood.

"You?" Gloria asked skeptically.

Jake forced a smile. "Scary thought, huh?"

Gloria got up and began the preparations.

Chapter 22

It was nine o'clock when the big man turned off Avon and parked on Martin Street. He locked his car, adjusted his long coat, and started walking back one block to Eaton's apartment building. He kicked at the leaves, the playfulness belying his intense concentration. His eyes darted about in the dark, his throat suddenly drier than usual.

For a moment, he had a painful glimpse of his future gone bad. Instead of anonymous freedom, he would be caught. Only this time there would be no grand scheme to protect the family.

Make no mistake. It wasn't he who was saved those many years back, it was the family's reputation, the family's future. Siblings couldn't survive with a scandal the size of the Boston Strangler hanging from their necks. No way. Doors would be shut to them, invitations not offered. That was no way to live, as some discovered when their own tarnish dimmed the family glow with infidelities and questionable money practices. Another scandal couldn't be survived. So now it was his turn to play savior; his turn to protect the reputation and future of his clan.

A barking dog brought him back to the moment. He turned around. An elderly, white-haired woman came walking out of the shadows with her leashed mutt. The big man smiled a greeting. He tipped an imaginary hat. It was what one normally did in the presence of the elderly. It was how one behaved, and he was good at acting. That's how you stay alive in this business. You act, you become a chameleon. He passed the old lady, then turned down the walk toward Jake's apartment.

The big man stood a moment inside the alcove breathing in the resonance of the building. He found Eaton's apartment number and rang the intercom buzzer long and hard, making certain that Jake was not at home. He was about to try the door when movement on the other side of the glass door startled him.

A middle-aged man carrying a laundry basket opened his apartment door and stepped into the entryway. He looked pleasantly at the big man. "Can I help?" he asked, shifting the basket under his arm.

"I don't think so. Just here to see a man on business. Doesn't appear to be in."

"Ahhh. You must mean Jake. He's the only one lucky enough to work at home. He's usually off on weekends. Sailing, last I heard."

"Sailing?"

"Some life, huh?"

"Yeah," the big man said, relieved. He was not looking for a fight—just Vicki Shaw. He was convinced that Eaton could lead him to her.

When the laundry basket disappeared down the walk, the big man took out a wire key. He inserted it into the Medeco lock, working it until the cams lined up, then opened the door. Upstairs he did the same to the lock on Jake's apartment door. He entered the dark hush of the hallway.

Closing the door behind him, he stood for a moment getting accustomed to the space. Light from a street lamp pouring through one window provided a slash of brightness in what looked like an office. The big man entered without delay and began his search.

After a dinner, graciously prepared by Gloria, of linguine with clam sauce, toasted garlic bread, salad, and fresh pineapple for dessert, Jake and Vicki sat around the table in the main salon. Grayish light from Vicki's laptop mixed with the soft glow of cabin lights bouncing off *Gamecock*'s varnished interior. Gloria was on deck checking dock lines and tightening the halyards for a quiet night's sleep. Watson was in the cockpit crunching on the hard ends of the toasted French loaf with the zeal normally reserved for a bone.

Jake sipped his brandy, staring at the words on the computer screen. Vicki had files of manuscript drafts, notes, and research similar to Drummond's. Unlike Drummond's, Vicki's were more complete, more methodical. "It's not hard to tell which one of you is the Harvard student," Jake said. "You even have an index."

"It's more like a basic cross-reference, but it works," Vicki said, explaining that she organized the data to save time because it matches how the Ebberhardt Institute arranges its files. "Only I don't incorporate the security restrictions," she said.

Jake wanted to know more and quickly. Vicki gave him the short version. Because of the sensitivity of data stored at the Ebberhardt Institute, restrictive security measures were adopted for everyone's use. Not that everyone could use the institute. Admission was limited to graduate students researching approved topics, qualified researchers not affiliated with Harvard, and law enforcement agencies.

"I take it," Jake said, "that a private detective couldn't just walk in and snoop around."

Vicki smiled at the thought. "You take it right," she said. "You wouldn't get past the front desk. Even if you did, you couldn't work the system. You need computer access to do that," Vicki said, her attention drawn to the gentle rocking of the boat.

"It's just Gloria securing the vessel," Jake reassured. "If it were anything else, Watson would let us know. Now, tell me more about the Ebberhardt."

"Why?"

"Because Drummond was curious about Walter Ebberhardt. Now I am, too. I think a look around the institute is in order."

Vicki looked at Jake as if she were scolding a child. "Didn't you hear what I just said? You can't get into the system. It's impossible."

"Not a word I like to use," Jake said. "I want you to get me into the Ebberhardt. You've got to figure out a way."

"I don't know that I can," Vicki said.

"Then," Jake said, dismissing her doubts, "I want you to tell me what to expect once I get inside."

"You can expect to get kicked out!"

"Maybe," Jake said. "Look, Vicki, Albert DeSalvo may have started this mess, but he's not around to finish it. It looks like I've been elected. Now, fill me in on the institute, so I don't make a fool of myself when I walk in the front door."

The Ebberhardt Institute was a solid, two-story, red brick building with white Doric columns framing the front. It was surrounded by manicured lawns and towering chestnut trees. Jake looked up at the tall, narrow windows on the imposing structure and thought that this is what a research institute ought to look like. When he entered the foyer, he thought it even smelled like a research institute: waxy, dusty, and slightly sweaty.

An impeccably dressed young man with the last name of Olgivy stamped on a plastic name tag sat behind a curved wooden desk in the main lobby. His thin shoulders slumped forward, his tortoiseshell glasses hung low on his long nose, and his face held a strained, unhappy expression.

The best time to gain entry, Vicki had counseled Jake, would be moments before closing. Institute staff are instructed to get everyone out by eleven with no exceptions. A disruption of the staff's routine might give Jake the advantage he would need to get inside, albeit for a brief time. But some time was better than none.

Jake walked up to the young man whose look grew increasingly impatient and annoyed with each step. Here it was fifteen minutes before closing and someone was going to ask for assistance.

"Sorry to bother," Jake said with a slightly British accent. "I was in earlier this morning and may have left one of my folders behind. Can't find it anywhere. Important material inside, you understand. Has anyone turned it in?" he asked, squinting at the plastic name tag. "Have you seen it, Mr. Olgivy? My name would be on it: Professor Willingham, University of London. Victor Willingham," Jake said through a toothy grin.

Olgivy's head moved ever so slightly. "Sorry," he said. "Nothing's come to the front desk. Not while I've been here."

"And when was that?" Jake asked, hoping the man worked the late hours.

"I come on at five."

"Oh, dear," Jake said, relieved that what Vicki had said about staff changes so far rang true. "I'm back to New York in the morning and then off to London. If I hurry, I can look up what I need in five minutes. Maybe less." Again Jake was all smiles. "Trouble is, my access card was in that folder. Professor Ebberhardt thoroughly explained your security to me—the different levels of access and all that—but he also said spare cards were available at this desk in cases of emergency."

"When did the professor tell you this?" Olgivy asked suspiciously.

"When he gave me my tour," Jake said, purposefully omitting when the supposed tour was given. Jake held up his wrist so his watch was clearly visible. "Please. I've come all this way. We're running out of time. Don't you make some concessions for emergencies?" Jake asked, already knowing the answer.

Reluctantly, an access card appeared on the counter. Jake scooped it up and dashed through the double doors. Inside was just as Vicki had described it: a cavernous main room filled with long tables on which sat computer terminals. At this hour, the room was nearly empty. The few people who remained were packing up.

Jake pulled a chair in front of a screen. He inserted the plastic card and typed in the access code, remembering all Vicki had told him about working the three access levels of the system. So far, she'd been right about everything, from the eagerness of the desk help to close the building to how to finagle computer access for a limited time.

And time was limited. Quickly, Jake clicked on the search-by-name icon in level three, the highest security level. A blinking blank line appeared. He typed in the name Walter Ebberhardt. Instantly, Access Denied appeared on the screen. He typed Michael Reardon. The same Access Denied blinked in front of him. Doug Turner's name also got him nowhere.

"Damn," Jake mumbled, getting up. Like a British don, he strolled back out to the main desk and said firmly, "Mr. Olgivy, you gave me a toy. I'm excluded from level three. Now," Jake said stiffening, "I understand your concern. You don't know me. You don't want trouble. Neither do I. What I want is the research I came all the way from England to get. We have two choices: we can either call your maintenance staff and spend the night hunting down my lost folder," Jake bluffed, "or you can give me five minutes in level three. It doesn't matter to me, as long as I'm out early enough to catch my plane."

Olgivy's expression clouded. "Only Professor Ebberhardt permits access to three."

"I know that." Jake managed his best English pout. "Where do you think I worked all morning? Level three is the reason for my trip to the institute, damn it to bloody hell!"

Slowly, another card appeared on the desk. "Five minutes," Olgivy said stiffly. "Not a second more."

Back at the terminal, Jake inserted the new card and retyped the code. Turner's name was still blinking on the screen. He moved the cursor beside the name and clicked. This time it took, and a message scrolled below. It read: "Turner, Douglas, R.: Dominating, manipulative. Motivated to police work by the strong sense of control law enforcement provides. Emotionally unstable. Deemed unsuitable for admittance into police academy per KSM, 1971. Review scheduled in six months. Candidate cleared for admission, 1972 class Boston PD. Graduated. Assigned C. Nash. Left force RE: IA report 498874: shooting. Attorney M. Reardon defended. Press Enter to continue."

Michael Reardon?

Jake didn't stop to think. He pressed Enter and found himself reading a paragraph on Curtis W. Nash, retired with full pension. Reason: medical disability. At the bottom of the screen was another reference to Internal Affair's report number 498874. It read in part, "The shooting involving Officer Turner caused Officer Nash severe emotional trauma. Subject unable to perform active duty. Recommendation per KSM: Medical discharge with full benefits. Approved: EK."

EK? Jake wondered. EK?

He forced himself to drop it, to use his computer time more wisely. He moved the cursor to the insert box and typed in the name of Walter Ebberhardt. He clicked. Before the screen filled, Jake sensed someone behind him. He glanced over his shoulder. Olgivy returned the look.

"Time's up," Olgivy said.

"Just one more sec—"

"Sorry." He reached down to the keypad just as Jake asked about KSM.

Olgivy's brow furrowed. "Certainly you've heard of it," he said. "It's the test used for qualifying for any U.S. police academy," Olgivy said, shutting down the system. "It's the standard measure used in all fifty states."

"What's the K stand for?"

"The man who devised the test: Ellison Kitter. It's the Kitter Standard Measure. There's no more reliable evaluation for personal motivation and psychological stability. You've probably got something like it in England."

Jake's thoughts were on Ellison Kitter. EK, Jake thought. "Where?" he heard himself say. "Oh, yes." He stood, showing Olgivy one more British smile. "Yes, yes, we have that sort of thing in England. Yes, we do."

Chapter 23

The traffic back to Marina Bay was light, the parking lot near the docks nearly empty. Most of the pleasure boats still in the water were covered with plastic for winter. The lobster boats were tied up for the night, ready for a run at the traps in the morning.

Jake moved easily down the docks. The smell of the salt in the air soothed his jangled nerves, which were brought on by an overpowering sense of dread. It was one thing to speak of conspiracies, quite another to open one like some lab rat and dissect it. But that's what Jake was doing. He was peeling back the skin and muscle; he was scraping at the bony skull. The only problem was, he wanted to examine the brain and was having trouble getting inside.

Was the hard-to-find Walter Ebberhardt the key to all locks? Where was he? Why was he so hard to contact? Had Lori Churchwell found him, talked with him, and lured him back to Boston? Had he come back to kill again? And, Jake wondered as he moved along, why was there a secured file on him at the institute? What was brother Neil Ebberhardt hiding?

Jake quickened his pace, weary of all the questions. He would sew up his rat until he was better able to generate answers.

A light breeze mixing with the gentle roll of the water sent a few halyards tapping against the metal masts. The deep thudding sound of heavy line against a wooden mast came from *Gamecock*.

Gloria was sitting in the cockpit, a wool shawl wrapped around her shoulders. Watson sat near the boarding ladder, his attention on the footfall coming toward him. When he recognized his master, he hopped to the dock and dashed toward Jake, his body torquing out of control. At the second joyful bark, Gloria leaned over the coaming, motioning Jake to be quiet.

Jake signaled Watson to stop yapping, then came aboard with the happy dog. "What's up?" Jake asked in a low voice.

"Vicki's asleep," Gloria answered. "Been a long day for her. I let her have the forward cabin. It's quieter up there. I think she could sleep for forty-eight hours."

Feeling a little worn himself, Jake eased himself down on the seat beside Gloria. The reflection of a dock light rode the ripples in the harbor. Jake followed them with his gaze, calmed by their motion.

Gloria reached over and began to massage Jake's neck. "How'd it go at the institute?" she asked, her voice suggesting she wasn't looking for bad news about either Neil or Walter Ebberhardt.

Jake told her how well Vicki had coached him. "I even worked my way into the system."

Gloria wasn't surprised. "Find anything interesting?"

"I did," Jake said, rolling his head loosely. Gloria's thumbs were doing the trick. "An old Internal Affairs report linking Curtis Nash, Doug Turner, Ellison Kitter, and Michael Reardon. Seems that Turner never should've been a cop and proved it by shooting someone as soon as he got on the force."

Gloria was more interested in another name. "What about Walter Ebberhardt?" she asked, trying not to sound anxious.

"Nothing," Jake said. "I couldn't retrieve his file. Not enough time," he said, leaning into the massage, loving every second, not wanting it to end. "What do you know about Walter?"

"Not much," Gloria said. "He was the quiet type from what I gather."

"You never met him?"

"No. He'd settled in Utah or Washington years ago. I don't really know which western state, but he's out there somewhere."

"The black sheep of the family kicked out of state?" Jake joked.

"Nothing like that," Gloria said, moving her fingers down to Jake's lower back. "From what Neil says, Walter wanted to prove to their father that he could make it on his own."

"Did he?"

"Apparently so," Gloria said. "The sad part is, Neil Senior died of heart failure before Walter got to make his point. Neil's head of the family now, and like brothers sometimes do, he and Walter quarrel."

"About what?"

"Neil's never spoken of it," Gloria said. "That tidbit I picked up along the way."

"You gossip hound," Jake teased, reveling in the pleasure of a great back rub.

"I prefer to say I'm a good listener."

"Then listen to this," Jake said. "Work your magic across my shoulders and I'll reciprocate."

"Deal, but let's continue in a warm bed," Gloria answered, nudging Jake. "If you make it that far without falling asleep."

"Me?"

"You. Now, get up," Gloria said, pushing Jake to his feet.

Jake helped Gloria stow the cockpit cushions. Once she and Watson were down below, he quietly asked for the phone.

Gloria handed it up. "Who are you calling at this time of night?" she asked.

"Business."

"Oh?"

Jake motioned toward the front of the boat. "I'll tell you later. Don't want to wake Vicki."

Jake stepped aft past *Gamecock*'s wooden steering wheel. He was as far away as he could get without falling overboard when he made his call to Sergeant Frank Cowen.

"Glad you're still on graveyard," Jake said.

"Yeah, well, I'm not," Frank gruffed. "I've been on duty since this morning when Jan Rybicki turned up. What's this all about, Jake?"

"It's about this morning," Jake said, about to stretch the truth. "You were right, Frank. You leveled with me about Ruth Hill, and I held back what I know about Rybicki's murder. I want to straighten that out."

The fatigue left Frank's voice. "I thought you were dancing a fine line," Frank told him. "What have you got?"

Jake glanced toward the companionway. He didn't want to upset Gloria with his inquiries into a family Gloria knew and respected.

Still, he had to follow through with the name that Drummond had questions about.

"You should check out Walter Ebberhardt," Jake said.

"Ebberhardt?" Surprise caught in the sergeant's throat. "Ebberhardt of the—"

"That's the one, Frank. His brother is Neil Ebberhardt, director of the institute."

"And a prime suspect in a copycat killing? Get real," Frank scoffed.

Jake sighed. "The copycat is Ron Hoenig's line," Jake reminded him. "I heard Lieutenant Stellar announce to the press that Boston was being damn helpful supplying leads. What if those leads are bogus, Frank? What if hunting down a copycat is to keep Cambridge busy looking in all the wrong places? They shut you out on Ruth Hill; why trust Boston now?"

Frank was silent a moment. "You've got a wicked mind, Eaton," he eventually said as a compliment. "Unfortunately, it matches mine. I doubted Hoenig's motives, too. What's your interest in Walter Ebberhardt?"

"It was Drummond's interest," Jake said. "He was following pedigrees and money all the way back to the identity of the real Boston Strangler. I'm following the same trail."

"What do you want me to do?" Frank asked.

"See what you can find out about Walter. All I know for certain is that he's living out west. Utah or Washington, maybe."

"That narrows it," Frank chided. "Anything else?"

"There is," Jake said, thinking back to Michael Reardon. If he was involved in the cover-up, if he was a player on the home team, why would someone kill his wife? Something didn't fit. "I'd like for you to check out Michael Reardon. He's an attorney—"

"I know who he is," Frank said, as if Reardon were an unpleasant memory. "The guy will defend anyone if the price is right. The cause doesn't matter as long as the bucks are there."

"Yeah, well, look around with care," Jake warned. "Reardon's in tight with Hoenig. Get me what you can, and fast, eh, Frank?"

"I'll see what I can do," Frank said, then hung up.

Jake turned around to find Gloria standing in the companionway wrapped snugly in her robe.

"I get the feeling you're not being honest with me, Jake," she said softly.

Damn, Jake thought. She's heard every word. "How's that?" he asked, hoping he was wrong.

"You promised to reciprocate." Gloria tilted her head. "The back rub, remember?"

"Ahh," Jake brightened. "Yes, yes. Coming right up." Jake's step lightened as he went below.

The morning brought a warm autumn sun that filled the cockpit. Jake was the first one out, taking Watson for his morning stroll. When he returned, Vicki was sitting outside, soaking up the sun.

"I can't believe just a few days ago it was snowing," she said as Jake climbed aboard. "And that I was hiding in a little room in Newport."

And that your writing partner and roommate were among the living, Jake thought, saying nothing.

Vicki looked around at her new surroundings. "Do you think anyone can find me here?"

"If I thought so, we'd be somewhere else," Jake said, tending to Watson's breakfast. "Still, I don't want you out and about. Stay with the boat until I say otherwise. Fair?"

"Fair," Vicki said. "How long?"

"Until the killer's caught," Jake said, the aroma of coffee percolating from below. He popped his head through the hatch with a greeting for Gloria, who had everything in the galley under control. Jake took a seat across from Vicki. "What you told me about the institute was right on," he said. "Olgivy reluctantly gave me an access card, and I was on my way."

"I'd say you were very lucky," Vicki admitted, relieved.

"Luck's part of the game," Jake agreed. "It's what you do with it that counts. I'd say Professor Kitter had his share of luck as well, being associated all these years with Boston PD."

"His early research, you mean," Vicki said knowingly. "The Standard Measure is how Professor Kitter established his reputation. Are you familiar with it?"

"Parts."

Vicki took the cue and gave Jake the short version. "Simply put, the Kitter Standard Measure is a series of psychological tests devised to identify personality types. The more aggressive type A groupings are separated from the less aggressive type B groupings, and so on. Professor Kitter didn't stop there, however. His genius was to match a personality type with a task that both challenged and rewarded the person performing the job. When matched successfully, officers live healthier and happier lives, and police departments have less trouble with rogue cops."

"He must've had some kinks to work out," Jake mused.

"Most research does," Vicki said flatly. "But what are you referring to regarding Kitter's work?"

"Not a what," Jake corrected. "A who. Doug Turner, to be exact. He was a rogue cop who Professor Kitter admitted into the academy. I was wondering if you knew why," Jake asked.

Vicki shook her head. "No."

"All right," Jake said. "How about the academy itself. Do you know how the professor managed a connection with Boston PD for his research?"

"I do," Vicki said with a nod. "Boston was the control site for Ellison's early testing. To hear Ellison tell it, he had little support from the men in the department. They had no interest in becoming guinea pigs."

"Probably afraid they'd test poorly and lose their jobs," Jake said. "But somebody must have wanted that testing done or it never would have happened. Any idea who that was?"

Vicki nodded again. "Conrad Fowler," she said. "To hear Professor Kitter talk about those days, the attorney general was behind most innovations in the police department. Not so much because he was an altruist, but because he wanted to build a record in case he decided to take the next political step and run for Congress."

"Which he did," Jake added as Gloria came into the cockpit carrying a tray with orange juice. She handed glasses around. "We were just talking about Senator Fowler," Jake explained.

"Oh, Connie," Gloria said with the tone of the familiar. "A wonderful man. Not in the best of health nowadays."

"Do you know him?" Jake asked, not surprised if she did. Gloria's family connections put her in contact with everyone.

Gloria put down the tray and sat. "I've known him for a long time, ever since my mother died nearly thirty years ago. He was very kind during that period of my life, very supportive of my father. Connie had just recently gone through a similar tragedy himself."

Jake asked about it.

Gloria sipped her juice, trying to remember. "It had to do with a family boating accident up in Maine. I don't remember all the details, but I do remember that Connie's sister-in-law and two of her children died when the gas engine of an old runabout exploded and the boat sank. It devastated Conrad. I remember my father commenting that Conrad didn't seem likely to survive the loss, it rattled him so."

"But he did," Jake said.

"Yes, he did," Gloria said. "Conrad is not one to give up." Gloria smiled. "He's like you in that regard. He gets something in his head and he won't let it go. I only hope the strength of his will can work equal wonders this time."

"How's that?" Jake asked.

"A string of bad luck," Gloria said, her concern for Senator Fowler showing in her eyes. "First Conrad's sister died, then his operation. Connie's back in Boston convalescing. I visited him in the hospital. He's quite straightforward about it," Gloria said. "The long-term prognosis doesn't look all that promising. Which reminds me," Gloria added, not wishing to dwell on the unpleasant, "I promised to meet with my contractor around eleven. I'll need a ride back to my car."

"You got it," Jake said. "I want to stop by my place anyway."

"What about me?" Vicki asked as Gloria went below to get her things.

"I want you to spend more time with your computer," Jake said. "Something's in that manuscript that the killer wants kept secret. If you look harder, maybe you can discover what it is."

"But we've been through all that," Vicki protested. "There's nothing there."

"You found nothing," Jake said. "There's a difference. Use the index this time through. We've been concentrating on names. Maybe we should look at something else."

"Like what?" Vicki asked.

"Dates. DeSalvo was arrested in 1964. Doug Turner joined the force in 1972. Scout everything between those two dates and see what you come up with."

"That's an interesting approach," Vicki admitted. "What else do you hope might show up?"

"References to Walter Ebberhardt and trips he made to Boston during the period the Strangler was actively killing," Jake said soberly.

Vicki turned her head away, her expression a labyrinth of conflicting emotions. Jake picked up on it immediately.

"What is it?" he asked.

She exhaled a sigh of dread. In her moist eyes, Jake saw her darkest fears, but he couldn't name them. He asked again what was troubling her.

"I was remembering a conversation I had with Bruce when we first started working on our book," Vicki said finally. "His suspicions about the conspiracy began with Boston PD. Mine began with someone connected to Harvard. I thought then that it would be hard to win against either. Now," she said, "I don't care who's behind it."

"I don't believe that," Jake said.

"It's true, because the result is the same: you end up dead like the others." She looked up at Jake. "We can't win. I know we can't. The sad part is I don't care anymore."

"I do," Jake said.

Vicki's eyes narrowed into hard slits. "You get paid to," she shot back.

"I get paid to do the job, Vicki," Jake said stiffly. "My feelings about Jan Rybicki and her last moments with that monster, and Drummond in the cage with those dogs, are free. From what little I know about Jan, I would imagine she—like Drum—fought to the end." Jake let the thought settle. "You should try it. The blows are never felt as much when you fight back."

Chapter 24

The workday traffic had eased by the time Jake turned into the Commercial Wharf lot and stopped at Gloria's car. His thoughts had been on Vicki and her fractured nerves. Jake wondered if she'd pull herself together enough to be of some help. He hoped so.

Gloria had spent the trip into the city scratching notes on a pad and doodling boxy shapes. Ideas for the house, she'd said cheerfully, about to explain to Jake for the second time what she meant by forest green flat wall paint for the library.

"I've seen it in England," she said. "It's very British, like the dark green color I've seen on Jaguars and MGs."

"Without the shine."

Gloria looked up from her pad. "Are you teasing me?" she asked, poking Jake's ribs with the eraser end of her pencil.

He answered her with a kiss, interrupted by someone tapping on the passenger-side window. It was Wilkins, the marina's dock boy.

"Sorry, Miss Gorham," Wilkins said when the window was rolled down. "Somebody was just here to see you. Thought I'd let you know before I left on break."

Jake's trifling mood disappeared as Gloria asked who it had been.

Wilkins shrugged. "Don't know," he answered. "Said he was here about your house. Like you wanted, I told him you'd taken *Gamecock* to Maine."

"But it could have been my architect!" Gloria objected.

"It could have been someone else, too," Jake cautioned. "He said he'd drop something by your house," Wilkins added, taking a five from Jake for his good deed. He pocketed it and left. Gloria turned to Jake. "You don't understand," she said. "Stan's office is just down the street. I told him to stop by the boat when he had something about the second floor changes he wanted to show me." Gloria grabbed her purse. "I'd better go call." She jerked open the car door. "Don't forget my skirt." She pointed to the blue silk number hanging from the travel hook in the backseat. "Hello? Jake, are you there?"

"I am," Jake said, his voice full of warning. "Be careful, Gloria. I don't want you getting hurt."

"Only if something falls on me in the house." The joke didn't change Jake's grim expression. "I'll be fine," she said, trotting off to her car.

Jake watched her get in, then drove back to his Martin Street apartment, convincing himself along the way that Gloria had been right. Her visitor at the marina was more than likely someone with business regarding her house. The ruse about the sail to Maine had only sent him to 28 Commonwealth Avenue to drop off something. It's what an architect would do. And a killer? He wouldn't even know about the house, Jake reasoned, feeling better.

He parked in front of his apartment building, then went inside. He was checking his mail when he remembered Gloria's skirt. She wanted it kept in his closet with her other things. Always something, Jake thought on his way back to the Saab. He had the skirt in his hand when he looked up and noticed that the green-shaded desk lamp in his office window had been left on.

He had not left it on. Of that he was positive.

He tossed his mail, and Gloria's skirt, inside the Saab and walked back across the street, thinking that whoever was looking for Vicki had paid a visit. Could he still be inside? Jake wondered, wishing all to hell that Watson were with him instead of on guard duty back in Marina Bay.

Jake missed Watson and his uncanny ability to sense danger seconds before Jake usually did. But this time Jake felt the presence of danger like an ache in a tooth. He opened the downstairs door, then took out his .38. He climbed the stairs, his eyes never leaving the top landing.

On the lock to his apartment door, he saw faint scratch marks. Someone had gotten in all right. Jake stepped to the wall and flattened his back against it. He took in a steadying breath, then tried the knob. The door was locked.

Without a sound, Jake removed the key from his pocket and slipped it into the lock. The bolt moved gently back and held. In what seemed like slow motion, Jake pushed open the door with the toe of one shoe. He bent at the knees and spun inside on the balls of his feet, his Smith & Wesson ready to fire.

On half steps, he turned into his office. Empty and wrecked. He moved quickly down the hall and into the living room. The same mess. The bedroom was torn apart in like fashion. The entire apartment had been opened like an eager child's Christmas present. Drawers hung open; papers, books, and clothes were everywhere but where they belonged.

Jake reholstered his gun and went back to his office. He sat at his desk and switched off the lamp. He imagined the intruder working the lock, then opening the door. Jake followed him into the office, opening file drawers just as the intruder would have. Jake knew that the intruder was looking for Vicki Shaw, or at least something that would lead him to her. Jake wondered what was here that would give the intruder that information. Jake hadn't left anything that would compromise her location. He was certain of that. But what about Vicki herself?

Jake went into his bedroom, where Vicki had slept. He hadn't noticed it the first time through, but tossed in the corner was one of the small nylon satchels that Vicki had brought with her. He picked it up. The zipper had been ripped open, the contents removed.

Back in the living room, Jake dialed *Gamecock*. When Vicki answered, he asked her about the satchel. She said she'd left it behind because those papers had nothing to do with her manuscript.

"What papers?" Jake asked.

"Parts of my dissertation," Vicki said haltingly. "Why? What's wrong?"

"The killer paid a visit," Jake said, explaining that his apartment had been ransacked and the contents of Vicki's satchel taken. "Where's Watson?"

"Right here beside me. He got to the phone before I did," Vicki said, attempting to lessen the tension.

"Don't get out of his sight," Jake cautioned, then asked her specifically about the contents of the satchel.

"As I said, a few dissertation chapters with Professor Kitter's written reaction to them. Part of his responsibility as my adviser is to provide detailed comment and direction," she said.

Jake asked about the nature of what Kitter had written.

"It wasn't terribly flattering, if that's what you mean. Ellison could be quite direct when he believed I was losing my focus. That was the case this time," Vicki said. "It seems I was letting some of my work with Bruce slip into my academic endeavors."

"How do you mean?" Jake asked.

"Flashy style, that sort of thing. Ellison said that my academic writing was getting soft, flowery. I kept the letter in the satchel as a reminder to keep the two projects separate. I also kept the most recent drafts—" Vicki stopped as it came to her like a lightning bolt. "My God, Jake! I kept the last chapters that Bruce had written about the Strangler in that satchel as well. I was going to read them, but then things got crazy," Vicki said.

"Then you never did read them?" Jake asked, as hopes for some help from her diminished again.

"No. Bruce gave them to me right after Lori Churchwell was murdered," Vicki recalled. "I had no stomach for anything." There was an awkward silence. "Maybe you're right," Vicki said. "Maybe I need to get up off the canvas and start swinging back."

I'd welcome it, Jake thought. He asked her where Kitter lived. If the Strangler had the contents of that satchel *and* the professor's notes, it wouldn't be much of a stretch for the killer to conclude that Kitter had read the chapters that Drummond had written. Kitter, Jake thought, could be in a hell of a lot of trouble.

Vicki gasped at Jake's question. "Oh, my God! Ellison lives out in the middle of nowhere!"

"Do you know where?"

"Yes. I've been there several times," Vicki said, and she rattled off directions.

Jake asked for Ellison's phone number. "Does he live alone?" Jake asked.

"No, his wife, Marti, lives there, too. If anything has happened to either one—"

"Let me worry about that," Jake told her, sensing her anguish through the phone. "Look, I know how you feel about Professor Kitter," Jake began, "but this is no time for heroics. Stay on that boat. Do you understand me?"

"I understand." Her voice was small and distant. "I want to know what happens," Vicki said. "I want to know if Ellison and Marti are all right."

"I'll call," Jake said, his thoughts already on his Smith & Wesson .44 Magnum.

He put down the phone and stepped to the hall closet. On the top shelf, he'd had built a secret panel for personal papers and the weapon he carried only when he wanted stopping power.

One shot from the .44 would stop a car. As he strapped on the gun, he hoped it would be enough to stop the man he now felt certain was the Boston Strangler.

Chapter 25

Ellison Kitter lived the life of a gentleman farmer fifteen miles from Boston in the town of Lexington, made famous by Paul Revere and his midnight ride. Jake raced there in minutes, picking up reckless speed when the Kitters failed to answer their phone.

At the Route 2 Shell station, Jake banked a right, fighting centrifugal force for control of the car. He leaned hard against the wheel, pulling it steady until the Saab straightened on the road. For five miles more on narrow blacktop, he sped by the homes of the gentry: white clapboard colonials with huge chimneys, sloping lawns with mature maples growing inside split-rail fences, a Mercedes or two in the drives.

Jake paid scant attention, his mind focused on keeping the old Saab on the curvy road. Half an hour from his apartment, he was sliding onto a gravel drive so long he couldn't see the house at the other end. Vicki said Ellison and Marti Kitter lived in that unseen house.

Jake downshifted into first and slowly followed the drive behind a cluster of white birch trees. Twenty yards behind the trees and more dense landscaping stood a saltbox colonial painted barn red. Jake stopped. He surveyed the property for signs of trouble, saw none, then drove on toward the garage.

The garage doors were open. Two cars were inside. Jake shut off the Saab's engine and got out. He moved cautiously toward the front door, his senses picking up the faintest detail, but nothing seemed out of the ordinary. At the front of the house, he peeked through a window with a parted curtain. The dining room was furnished in antique pine complete with trestle table and pie safe. Jake saw nothing suspicious.

He tried the bell. He rang it once, waited, then rang it again. When no one came to the door, Jake started around back. He made it to the side of the house, where he could look in another set of windows. He found one with a shade partially up and looked inside.

The living room furniture was in place, yet Jake had the uncanny feeling that something terrible had happened nearby. He couldn't explain it. He certainly hadn't seen anything that dictated such a response, but it was all around him like some penetrating numbness.

On instinct, Jake dashed around back and up a set of redwood stairs to the deck. The back door was locked, but not for long. Jake pulled his Magnum and broke the side light. He reached through the shattered glass and turned the lock.

He stood quietly in the back hall, listening to what the old house could tell him. Whatever it was, it didn't change his mind. Something was wrong.

Once Jake's eyes adjusted, he moved through the kitchen with its floor-to-ceiling windows on the south side. Outside, an empty bird feeder swayed in the light breeze.

Jake moved into the hall taking slow, cautious steps. At the stairway to the second floor, he called out. No one answered back.

The wooden stairs creaked underfoot. Jake climbed them like a man wading in surf. The only difference was that he held a small cannon, not a fishing rod.

When he made the hall, Jake headed for the closed door across from him. He sensed that he was about to open it on something he'd never experienced before.

With one hand, Jake raised the .44. He cocked it, then reached down for the knob. He turned it and swung the door open. The empty office was ransacked.

Jake felt his pulse quicken as his eyes darted around the chaos. Where are the Kitters? he wondered. With one step, he backed out of the office. Down the hall was a second closed door. Without hesitating, Jake threw it open.

"Goddamn," he heard his own voice say as he saw the two bodies. The woman was nude and waxy pale. She'd been propped up on pillows so she sat, legs spread facing Ellison Kitter. A red scarf had been tied in a bow around her neck, the ends falling below her lolling breasts. From the bruises and small reddish welts around her thighs, Jake could tell she'd been raped.

Jake put away his revolver. He stepped carefully around Ellison, who sat fully clothed, arms behind him tied to the slats of the arrow-backed chair. Jake fought a jittery feeling. He'd never been able to acquire an indifference to death, especially when the innocent were involved.

What had Marti Kitter done to deserve this? Jake wondered. What could any woman have done to suffer a rape while her husband—tied to a chair not five feet away—looked on? Ellison must have gone through hell, Jake thought getting closer to the man.

Ellison had been shot execution style in the back of the head with a small-caliber weapon. His wrists were cut where he'd struggled against the rope before dying. Death must have been a relief, Jake thought, his own feelings of contempt and hatred for the rapist boiling within.

Something about Ellison's wound was wrong, Jake observed, examining the exit hole more closely. Ellison's head was leaning forward and to the right. The angle of Ellison's head wouldn't produce the amount of blood that was caked on his left cheek. It was physically impossible. All the blood should have run to the right, the direction his head tilted.

Jake bent at the knees for a closer look. A frigid wash ran through him as he observed the raw, uneven line running across the upper back portion of each eyeball, leaving the eyes exposed and wider than normal. The lids had been cut away, producing a stream of blood that ran down from the corner of each incision, caking on the cheeks.

Ellison Kitter had been unable to close his eyes while his wife was being raped.

A crush of emotion knotted inside Jake. He turned his back to the bodies, moving in slow motion as if a bomb would explode from any quick move. His eyes locked on an envelope leaning against the lamp on a dressing table.

The envelope had Jake's name on it.

Tension wormed its way up his spine as he reached out and picked it up. Slowly, he tore open the flap, exposing two newspaper clippings the Strangler must have taken from Jake's apartment.

One was a grainy photograph of Jake and Gloria at the opening-night party for the Boston Symphony. The second was a piece on the renovations Gloria had planned for the house at 28 Commonwealth Avenue. A folded paper contained the hand-written message: "I'm bored with chasing Vicki Shaw. You will bring her to me if you ever hope to see Gloria Gorham alive. And, Eaton, no cops. If I get the smell of one, Gloria dies. Time and place coming. Be ready."

A knot caught fire in Jake's stomach. "The man at the marina!" he muttered, hurrying downstairs to the phone. Jake grabbed the receiver and frantically punched in some numbers. By now, Gloria must be at the house. The dock boy said the man looking for her at the marina would go there next.

"Come on, come on, come on," Jake repeated, coaxing Gloria to answer her cellular phone. When she did not, Jake bolted to his car.

He gripped the steering wheel as he wrestled with the road. The old Saab was humming at ninety on a stretch of highway built for horse-drawn buggies. As the asphalt sped by, Jake felt his frustration rising, knowing he could never reach the house in time, knowing he didn't dare call the police. If the police made it to the house, Jake feared the Strangler would be true to his word and kill Gloria on the spot. He would not take the chance.

No, his only chance was to drive like hell and hope for a lot of luck. Maybe Gloria stopped off somewhere. Maybe she ran some errands and got stuck in traffic. Jake could imagine a thousand possibilities, but the most likely was that Gloria hurried to catch the architect before he left the house.

Jake pressed his foot harder on the accelerator and closed in on Boston.

Chapter 26

Construction sites are like open wounds. All you have to do is walk around long enough to find an entrance, then go inside. Plumbers, electricians, carpenters locked nothing until the end of the workday. They threw the doors open and got down to the business of soldering, wiring, and hammering away.

The big man had been in the house since leaving Commercial Wharf earlier in the morning. He'd parked in the alley, had a careful look around, then went inside. He walked around holding a clipboard, looking serious, doubtful. When he felt a curious glance come his way, he'd scratch a note on the pad. The looker would turn away as if guilty.

The big man went to the basement, biding his time. He was alone down there, out of the way of others. When the time was right, he came upstairs with the bad news: one of the abutting neighbors complained of water seeping into their basement since Miss—whose renovation project is this? Right, right, Gorham—since Gloria Gorham started work on this project. Got to check it out. Is she around? Well, somebody here ought to put a call in. Tell her to get right over. Yeah, I'll wait. That's why I'm here.

Gloria was already on her way, so the big man didn't have to wait long to hear her apologies. She knew the Back Bay was built on landfill, the old town houses supported by wooden pilings driven deep into the wet ground. Some sort of water damage was possible. Could she see the basement? See how bad the damage was? Talk to her neighbors, maybe? Gloria didn't want trouble.

The big man hoped she'd be so agreeable. In fact, the neighbors were waiting. Shall we go?

Jake screeched to a stop in front of number 28, got out, and ran up the worn granite steps. He burst through the door with a vengeance, looking frantically for any sign of Gloria.

"Is she here?" he snapped at the first worker he saw.

"Who?" the man asked without interest.

"Gloria, you idiot!" Jake said savagely, then brushed past the man and up the stairs. He didn't get far when he was told the news: Gloria had left more than an hour ago with the inspector. The informer had no idea what was taking so long, but she should be back soon.

The words rang in Jake's ears. He wanted to believe they were true. Gloria would be back soon. Yes, she would. But only if Jake made it happen.

The Strangler had come back to guarantee that his identity remain secret, that the conspiracy of silence remained mute. Gloria's voice would have to be silenced if the Strangler were to succeed. Jake would not let that happen. He would do whatever it took to get Gloria back. That was all there was to it: he would get her back.

Jake got to his car and opened the door on a ringing phone. His heart about to explode, he picked it up. "Yes?"

"Eaton?" His name came through the phone on a dark, throaty voice.

"Yes. Who's this?" Jake asked, knowing the answer.

"The man with your lady." There was a moment's silence, then Gloria's voice gasped into the phone. "Jake? Jake, I'm so sorry, I—" There was a quick scream of agony. More silence followed, then the man's voice came back on. "I take it you found the envelope."

"Listen, you—"

"No. You listen." The man's voice was deadly serious. "I want Vicki Shaw."

"She can't do anything for you," Jake said.

"I *want* Vicki Shaw," the big man repeated as another anguished scream from Gloria seeped through the phone.

Jake felt the receiver tremble slightly in his fingers. He gripped it tighter to steady it and himself. "I'll find her," Jake said.

"You'll do better than that. You'll bring her to me. Understand?"

Jake understood who was calling the shots. "Yes," he said, hunting for an advantage. The man on the other end of the phone had them all, except one thing: Jake was nearly certain he knew the man's identity. Jake wanted to blurt out: Aren't you Walter Ebberhardt? But he held back. He knew that even when fragments start to fit, they are still only fragments. The clear, certain picture lies up ahead. This is not a time to be recklessly guessing the Strangler's identity. Not with Gloria's safety hanging in the balance on a life-and-death teeter-totter. Jake took in a short breath and asked when Vicki was to be delivered.

"Tomorrow at four o'clock," the big man said.

"I may need more time," Jake said, stalling.

"Three o'clock," the man said gruffly. "I know every game, Eaton. Don't play with me. I'm tired of playing."

Jake heard the seriousness and asked where they should meet.

"When I'm ready, I'll let you know." The man paused, then said, "You'll have plenty of time to get there."

"I'll be ready."

"So will I."

"Let me speak to Gloria."

"Tomorrow, Eaton." The phone went dead.

Jake looked at his watch. It was just after noon.

Chapter 27

The world is full of surprises mixed with a dash of chaos. Harvard types may spend years analyzing such a statement, trying to verify it. Jake, however, knew its truth instinctively. It was part of his job, part of his view of the world.

Rolling along with the good times can lead to a dangerous feeling of confidence, as if you've somehow beaten the odds. Chaos skipped your apartment and moved in next door. But it will be back, knocking. Wanting in. Seeping through the cracks, hovering around unseen like a hawk riding an updraft.

Jake's emotional ride came from Gloria's abduction. But he flattened it, knowing that unchecked emotion had no place in solid detective work. Instead, he directed his energy toward finding Neil Ebberhardt. Jake wanted to talk with him now. But he got no answer at home, and only voice mail at the institute.

Vicki Shaw's emotional chaos came from the phone call Jake had promised. He'd left 28 Commonwealth Avenue, driving through his anger and Boston's potholed streets, the steering wheel shaking like a house in an earthquake.

He had picked up the phone, gambling on some strength within Vicki that he had never witnessed. He told her the truth about the deaths of Ellison and Marti Kitter. He masked the horror in a half whisper, but he did not try to disguise the facts.

Vicki took the news, then howled with the force of dynamite bursting through her vocal cords. A silence followed. Hiccuping sobs. A struggle for breath.

When Jake boarded *Gamecock,* he expected to find Vicki collapsed in grief, destroyed, helpless. Instead, she was sitting before her laptop like some woodcarving, staring at the greenish screen. Jake welcomed the surprise. He moved past the attentive Watson and sat beside Vicki. He put his arm across her back. "I'm sorry," he said.

Vicki shivered. Her head ticked left, then right in a shake of denial. Speaking of death made it somehow more real. There were other things to think of, things that cluttered the mind, things that let you continue.

Jake knew that game. It worked for a little while like some drug, but eventually reality won out and you crashed like the '29 stock market.

Jake shifted to the settee across from her. Watson followed, nosing for attention. Absently, Jake stroked the black dog's wide head. "The Strangler's got Gloria." he said gravely.

Vicki cut Jake a look as if some fear in her had been newly awakened.

"I need you to help me get her back," Jake told her.

Vicki's expression darkened. "He wants to trade, doesn't he? He wants you to hand me over."

"Yes," Jake admitted. "But that's not going to happen."

"What is?"

Jake felt the blood drumming at his temples. "We're going to catch the Boston Strangler," Jake said. "We're going to get Gloria out of there."

"You sound just like Bruce Drummond," Vicki commented ruefully, the memories of Bruce coming alive.

Jake didn't have time for that reality to dull Vicki's mood. He had neither the time nor the patience. "I told you once," he said brusquely, "I was hired to do this job, and that's what I'm going to do. It'd be a hell of a lot easier if you'd work with me."

"As if I haven't been," she said, her head bobbing toward the small computer. "Professor Kitter once paid me the greatest compliment. He said I had the makings of a fighter, of someone who could come out on top if I stayed the course." Vicki's eyes filled. She flicked away a tear scudding across her cheek. "Well," she said defiantly, "I have no intention of giving in. I won't disappoint you, Mr. Eaton, or myself. In fact, I may have a place for us to start."

Jake sneaked a sigh of relief. "Where?" he asked.

"My office," Vicki said.

Jake shook his head. "No way."

"But my dissertation files are there on another computer," Vicki protested.

"So?"

"So, we need information, Jake. There's no network connection from this boat to my office. We have to go and have a look at those files. They might answer some questions that this computer can't." There was a pause, then Vicki added, "I know you want me here for my protection, Jake, but I can't help you if we stay."

"All right," Jake said, picking up the phone. "But let me try Neil Ebberhardt one more time."

Chapter 28

Lehman Hall is a yellow clapboard building on one end of Harvard Yard. Jake, Vicki, and Watson—not the first prohibited dog on the premises—climbed the front stairs and hurried inside.

There were two dining rooms and several small, cramped offices on the first floor. On the mezzanine, past two grand pianos, were a computer room and a spacious student lounge complete with television and pool tables. A library occupied all of the third floor.

Jake quickly followed Vicki to the fourth floor. Through massive double doors, down a hall where portraits of dead Harvard alumni hung from white walls, they finally came to Vicki's office.

Vicki unlocked the small sanctum brightened by windows overlooking the Yard. She sat behind her desk, which was stacked dangerously high with loose piles of paper. The desk reminded Jake of Vicki's apartment and Jan Rybicki's torturous death. The idea that Gloria could be next knifed through him.

A computer workstation sat in the corner. Vicki spun her chair to the computer and switched it on. "This might take a while," she said when Jake asked what she was looking for. Vicki explained how her dissertation began with establishing a baseline of male serial killers' behavior.

"I remember," Jake said. "Albert DeSalvo didn't fit that profile."

Vicki worked at the keyboard as she spoke. "That's right," she said. "But if I'm correct, there's another killer who does fit but who I didn't include in my baseline because I had no data on him."

"Why's that?" Jake asked.

"Because he was never categorized as a serial killer," she said, her attention fixed on the screen. "He didn't kill with the frequency needed to be labeled a serial killer. His victims showed up randomly as if he'd escaped from prison from time to time. Only trouble was, no prison escape was ever reported. But," she turned to Jake, "he did rape and strangle his victims."

"What about the bow around the neck of the victims?" Jake asked uneasily, as if he already knew the answer.

"Yes," Vicki said. "Around each victim's neck was tied a bow."

"What else did you find out about him?" Jake asked.

Vicki shook her head. "Nothing on the laptop. I'll have to check this system to see what I can pull up. But there's something else I want to dig into," she said. "Those dates you wanted me to scan, 1964 to 1972. Two names popped up in 1972: Albert DeSalvo and Doug Turner. That was the year Turner was sent to prison and the year De-Salvo was killed behind bars."

Jake felt as if he'd just been handed a surprise gift. "Were they in the *same* prison?" he asked.

Vicki gestured to her computer. "The answers are in there somewhere."

"You've got as much time as it takes me to talk with Neil Ebberhardt," Jake said, glancing at his watch. "He promised to meet me in front of the library in five minutes." Jake bent down to Watson and scruffed his neck. "You're in charge, pal," he said, moving out the door. "We've lost one lady; let's not make it two."

Jake walked by Thayer House and the other stately brick Harvard dorms. Straight ahead stood Harvard's Widener Library, a mass of granite, columns, and wide, imposing stairs.

Neil Ebberhardt stood on the bottom step, his hands in his gray suit coat pockets, his dark brown eyes fixed thoughtfully on some point in space. He had a medium build and a wide face and nose. There was something kingly about him, something very proper. Or was it arrogance? Jake wasn't sure, but he was about to find out.

"What's this about Gloria being in trouble?" Ebberhardt asked, his concern apparently genuine.

"Your brother may have the answer to that," Jake said bluntly.

Ebberhardt didn't flinch. "My brother?" The professor seemed to weigh his options, which Jake imagined hovered somewhere between hope of escape and nightmare. "Mind if we walk?" He did not wait for an answer.

They crossed Massachusetts Avenue and past one of Cambridge's many outdoor cafes. The bright sun warmed the afternoon enough to entice a few students to eat outside.

"I don't have a lot of time, professor," Jake reminded him, following Ebberhardt across Bow Street. "Gloria has less."

"I will do what I can to help, of course," Ebberhardt said, a curl to his upper lip. "Although I don't really see—"

Jake cut him off with an informational bomb. "Marti and Ellison Kitter are dead," Jake told the professor.

"Dead?" He looked stunned. His eyes narrowed to slits, as if understanding were beyond his comprehension. "Why haven't I heard anything?"

"You will soon enough," Jake said, explaining that he'd found the bodies earlier in the day and notified the authorities. "The Lexington police will release nothing until the state boys tell them to."

Ebberhardt seemed locked in place, his jaw tightly set. "I can't believe it," he said, bringing his hands to his temples. "Marti and Ellison."

"Added to your brother's list," Jake said indignantly.

Ebberhardt lowered his hands and looked impudently at Jake. "What are you suggesting?" he asked, making the shabby connection. "You don't for one minute believe that Walter had anything to do with this."

"A minute's about what I'm going to give you, professor," Jake told him. "Where's your brother right now?"

"How should I know?"

"You mean he didn't call when he got back to Boston?" Jake prodded.

"That's preposterous!" Ebberhardt snapped. "What evidence have you that he's in town?"

"A trail of bodies," Jake answered as Ebberhardt quickened his pace. "You can't run away, professor. Even if you tried, I'd be standing in your shadow."

Jake reached out with one arm and caught Ebberhardt's shoulder. The professor stopped, his expression a mingling of guilt and relief. Slowly, he took in his surroundings as if seeing them for the first time. He pulled in a lung full of air to quiet his jangled nerves. "It's not what you think," he said finally.

"Convince me."

"I don't know that I can," Ebberhardt admitted bitterly, "if you have the same agenda as Vicki Shaw and that reporter friend of hers."

"You spoke to Drummond?" Jake asked.

"Yes. Not that he listened to reason, but I did speak to him."

They crossed to Arrow Street. Behind them the spire on St. Paul's Church rose into the clear blue October sky.

"Drummond thought your brother might be involved in the Strangler case," Jake offered. "He thought he might even be the Strangler. Is he?"

"Of course not."

"But," Jake said, "neither was Albert DeSalvo. Was he." It was not a question.

"My reputation—the Ebberhardt Institute itself—is based on my identification of Albert DeSalvo as the Boston Strangler." The professor looked wearily at Jake. "Do you have any idea what it would mean if I answered that question?"

"It will mean Gloria's life if you don't," Jake answered. "It's past time for appearances, professor. I need answers no matter who or what they hurt."

Ebberhardt nodded. It was as if he had finally agreed that any attempt at subterfuge was pointless. The realization made him seem a little queasy. He shoved his hands back inside his coat pockets. "My father was a pillar of the community," he said. "A little extreme in his opinions, perhaps, but an Ebberhardt to the core: solid, noble, good upbringing, and—unfortunately—a drunk. In his middle years, drinking became his profession. He hid it well. Worked at it. Kept it from everyone except his family. Father was hardest on Walter. Walter didn't take it well and got into some trouble with women."

"What kind of trouble?" Jake asked.

"The physical kind," Ebberhardt admitted sadly. "Walter was an abuser. He took out his frustrations on any woman who'd put up with him. But," he said, looking firmly at Jake, "Walter never killed any-one. I explained that to Bruce Drummond, but he'd run across some court records linking Walter to a woman he'd beaten rather badly."

"She brought charges?" Jake asked.

Ebberhardt nodded, his expression like stone. "Yes. Drummond tried to make more of it than the facts suggested."

"Then," Jake said accusingly, "is that why your brother came back and killed him?"

"He didn't! Walter has disowned his own family," Ebberhardt blurted. "He didn't even come back for Father's funeral. He ignores us, shuns us."

That could explain, Jake thought, why Lori Churchwell had trouble contacting Walter Ebberhardt: he simply didn't care enough to respond. It could also explain Walter's closed file at the institute. But it didn't explain who had Gloria. If it wasn't Walter Ebberhardt, who the hell was it?

Jake clenched his fists and took in a steadying breath. It was time for discipline, not self-pity. It was time to learn the truth, and Neil Ebberhardt had it—at least some of it.

"This is important, professor," Jake said, "It isn't like your work on some board, or your committee interest in the Boston Symphony. This is Gloria's life we're talking about, damn it! And Vicki Shaw's, if I screw up." Jake let the message gain weight. "Were Vicki and Drummond right about the Strangler not being Albert DeSalvo?"

Ebberhardt cast his eyes about as if hunting some way back to safe ground.

"Were they?" Jake pressed.

Ebberhardt folded his arms across his chest and sat down on a brick retaining wall. He looked Jake straight in the eye as if finally resigned. "Yes," he said. "When I heard what Vicki Shaw was actually working on at the institute, I restricted her use. I had hoped she would get discouraged and go back to her dissertation. I hadn't counted on her being partners with a tenacious reporter."

"Who was about to uncover the real identity of the Boston Strangler," Jake added.

"Yes," Ebberhardt said, as if it no longer mattered.

"Who is he?" Jake asked, conscious he was holding his breath. "Who has Gloria?"

Ebberhardt shook his head, his face dark and flat. "It's important you understand that I did what I had to do," he said. "Thirty years ago, I had no choice but to match DeSalvo's characteristics with those of a serial killer." He swallowed hard, his eyes clear as ice. "I had to, you understand. My brother could have gone to prison if I didn't go along."

Jake stood stiffly, his disgust growing. "Who threatened you?" he demanded.

The professor's fingertips were trembling. "Conrad Fowler," he said dully. "He gave me an ultimatum: identify someone as the Boston Strangler soon or Walter will stand trial. All of Walter's past indiscretions would be made public. The chance of his conviction was nearly certain, the ruination of our family equally so."

"So you picked DeSalvo?"

Ebberhardt nodded. "He was no saint," he said, as if honor had suddenly come to his side. "Besides, my work was very new then. I'd been trying for months to identify the Strangler and couldn't do it. It *could* have been DeSalvo."

"Could it really?"

Ebberhardt swallowed, then turned his eyes away. "No," he said. "I've regretted it every minute of every day. The Strangler wasn't De-Salvo, and I knew it."

Jake's thoughts jumped over Ebberhardt's regret onto something more puzzling. If DeSalvo wasn't the Strangler, why did the killings stop once he was arrested? Ebberhardt must have been assured that they would stop, or naming Albert DeSalvo as the murderer of thirteen women would have make him a laughingstock.

"What guarantees did you have that there would be no more killings?" Jake asked.

Ebberhardt brightened. "That's the point, you see. That's how I've lived with myself all this time. Conrad swore to me that justice was being done, that the real Strangler was being punished to the full extent of the law."

"And you bought that?" Jake said, not hiding his distaste.

"I bought my brother's life," Ebberhardt snapped back. "Everything would have been fine had Bruce Drummond not come poking around. I knew it was the end of what I'd worked for all my life, so I announced my retirement from the institute." The professor's eyes narrowed on Jake. "I know it isn't enough. I know nothing will ever be, but, please! Don't let Gloria become the next victim. I couldn't live with myself knowing things had come this far."

"Tell me who the Strangler is," Jake said bluntly.

"Do you think I'd keep that from you if I knew?" Ebberhardt's eyes were fiery. "Think what you want, but I'm not a monster."

"No," Jake said bitterly. "You just let one get away."

Chapter 29

The big man sat at the table, hands folded like a steeple. Across from him, bound and gagged, Gloria held back the urge to cry. Such a display of emotion would gain nothing. She knew that and sat still, murderous thoughts flashing through her mind. She was strong. She was capable. Sailing had provided those lessons. She would fight the big man, fight back when he came for her. She would try to kill him if she had to. It was a terrifying thought, but if that was the only way . . .

"What are you thinking?" the big man asked, his voice filling the cramped space, startling her. It was a rhetorical question. He had no intention of removing the gag, of letting her speak. The big man laughed palely, his cruel eyes without compassion.

Gloria met his stare, understanding in that briefest moment the kind of courage and daring Jake displayed daily. It was as if she'd pulled back the curtain of some forbidden room and looked in. The sight frightened her. She closed her eyes.

A creak in the hall lifted her hopes. Was someone climbing the stairs? Had Jake found her? She strained to hear more, and heard nothing but wind rattling the windows.

The big man reached across the table and pulled the phone toward him. "Time to jangle the chain around Eaton's neck," he said with perverse joy. "Keep the boy off balance, running in circles."

Gloria's eyes asked the question.

He picked up the phone. "You'll see," he said, almost too softly to hear.

● ● ●

Jake brushed past students coming down the hall, then entered Vicki's office without knocking. She glanced up from her computer. "How'd it go with Ebberhardt?" she asked.

"It went nowhere," Jake said. "Walter Ebberhardt is a dead end."

Vicki went right back to work as if any interruption would be damaging.

Jake recognized the look. "What?" he asked, stepping hopefully around Watson. "What have you got?"

"A couple of things," Vicki said, eyes still on the terminal. "Turner and DeSalvo were in the same prison at the same time."

"Meaning that Turner could have killed DeSalvo," Jake added.

"It's possible. Second, those other stranglings I told you about? They all took place in Maine."

"Maine?" Jake repeated, trying to make some connection.

"That's right. I'm relying on Ruth Hill's records for most of this. I loaded her files on this system, too. All the research she did going through newspaper files is in here," Vicki said, pointing to her computer.

"What did Ruth dig up?" Jake asked.

"Something very interesting," Vicki said. "About a month before Lori Churchwell was found murdered, Sarah Fowler died at the Maine estate she owned with her brother, Senator Conrad Fowler."

"Senator Fowler?" Jake repeated suspiciously. "Gloria mentioned he had a sister but nothing about her. What have you got?"

From the print tray, Vicki handed Jake a copy of the obituary. Jake read it, learning that the never-married Sarah Anne Fowler, seventy-four, had dedicated her life to unpublicized philanthropy. From her home in the Fowler compound, she oversaw trusts that gave generously to the arts and education. When asked why she shunned publicity, she'd said once that having one Fowler quoted in the paper almost daily from Washington was enough. She'd died of injuries sustained from a fall in the home. The funeral was private. Burial was at the Maine estate where all the Fowlers were buried, except her brother Jay Brandon Fowler, whose body was never recovered from a boating accident.

Jake gave the page back to Vicki, his thoughts spinning. "The boating accident that Gloria mentioned? The one that happened more than thirty years ago?"

"That's the one," Vicki said. "I just had a file about it on the screen. There weren't many details, just that Jay Brandon died gallantly trying to save his wife and two children once their boat caught fire."

"What was the date?" Jake asked.

"It was 1964."

Jake felt a stab in his chest. "The year the Strangler killed his last victim in Boston."

Vicki sank back in her chair. "Are you saying the senator's brother is the Boston Strangler?"

"I'm saying I'd like to know more about Sarah Fowler's death and why—with all her millions—she spent most of her adult life hidden away in Maine. Think you can get that for me?"

"Sure," Vicki said.

"How soon?"

"Computers are *very* fast, Jake," Vicki said with a curt smile. "I'll start with Ruth's files, then go from there. How about yourself?"

"It's time I talked with Conrad Fowler," Jake said, moving purposefully toward the door.

Vicki called him back. "Jake?"

He turned and stopped.

Vicki's eyes were sad and serious. "I know it could be me with the Strangler, not Gloria. We'll get her back. I know it."

Jake's smile was quick. Just as quickly, he was out the door.

Chapter 30

On the way to Conrad Fowler's, Jake put in a call to Frank Cowen. Frank was off duty but had the information Jake requested. The news on Walter Ebberhardt was as stale as two-day-old bread. Frank said that Walter Ebberhardt may be a lot of things, but he wasn't in Boston doing any of them.

"Walter was seen on his ranch as late as yesterday," Frank said. "Do you want the kinky news on Michael Reardon?"

"Shoot," Jake said, wondering how kinky.

Frank told him. "Rumor has it that Reardon went off the deep end when he heard that a book was being written about the old Strangler case. He put word out that he wanted to get his hands on a copy before it went to press."

"You're saying he wanted to buy the manuscript?" Jake asked.

"That's what I'm saying," Frank agreed.

"He was probably afraid the book would ruin his practice," Jake said, recalling Drummond's conjecture that Michael Reardon was in on the conspiracy up to his knees.

"Better ruined than having your wife killed trying to save it."

The way Frank said it sent a chill down Jake's back. "What do you mean?" he asked. He could almost see Frank shrug his big shoulders.

"I mean that someone had made contact with Reardon. He didn't say he was the Strangler, just some schmuck with a manuscript to sell."

"And," Jake said, filling in the blanks, "he'd sell it only to Michael's wife, Sylvia."

"You got it."

"The sick, rotten bastard," Jake heard himself say. "We've got to get this guy, Frank."

"Yeah," Frank said. "You don't think he's a copycat, do you? You think the Boston Strangler is paying us another visit?"

"I do."

"Like he's come back from the dead or something. It's spooky, Jake. I've got a bad feeling about it," Frank said. "Real bad."

Not as bad as mine, Jake thought to himself.

"If I hear anything else, I'll call," Frank said and hung up.

Jake put down the phone. He hadn't removed his hand when it jingled again.

"That was fast, Frank," Jake said. "What'd you remember?"

"I've never forgotten it," the big man said, speaking like a cold functionary. "I stay one step ahead of those chasing me. I'm changing the rules, Eaton. Tomorrow's meeting has been moved up."

"What? Wait a second."

"You didn't *really* think I'd give you enough time to plan an offense, did you?" he said. "Not a chance. We meet today at six."

Jake glanced at his watch. It was three o'clock. "But—"

"No buts. Your lady friend likes to talk during sex. I suppose you know. She gets real chatty. I like that."

Jake's knuckles whitened as he nearly tore the steering wheel from the post. "You bastard!" he said, the heat of fire flashing through him. "If you've harmed one hair—"

"She's still alive," the man said, as if talking about weather. "She told me you've already got Vicki," the man said coolly. "You don't need time to track her down."

Through gritted teeth, Jake asked to speak to Gloria.

"Six o'clock today," the big man said. "I'll tell you where when I'm ready." Then he hung up.

Jake slammed down the phone, his thoughts with Gloria and the monster. By sheer force of will, he had to concentrate on the road while fighting through a kind of dizziness. He felt as if he'd stood too quickly and needed to grab hold of something to steady himself. What Jake wanted a hold of was the man with Gloria. In an irony Jake noticed, he wanted to strangle the bastard with his bare hands. He wanted to squeeze out his life. He wanted to do it now.

Instead, Jake tortured his Saab, sucking all the power he could from the engine as he blasted toward Senator Fowler's Beacon Hill home.

Conrad Fowler lived in a brick bowfront partway up West Cedar Street. It was one of those lovely town houses typical on the Hill that exuded the neighborhood's common quality: wealth. Fowler made no secret of his Boston address.

Jake skidded into the curb, shut off the engine, and got out. On the granite stoop, he rang the polished brass buzzer. In moments the door opened to the safety chain. A sturdy-looking woman in her mid-fifties wearing the uniform of paid help peered out. An introduction got Jake nowhere.

"Tell Senator Fowler I have news about his brother," Jake said, watching the door ease shut. After a while, it reopened without the chain.

The woman led the way across the hall into a room with a grand piano at the far end. Nearer to Jake was a seating arrangement of matching chintz sofa and chairs. The woman offered Jake a chair, then left as Conrad Fowler entered the room.

The senator—as Jake had remembered him from all those photo ops on television—was of medium height, slightly paunchy, with bulging eyes in a plump face. It was the eyes that Jake remembered most: they had been fiery black orbs, always bright, always looking for the next fight. Senator Fowler never ducked one, started many, and won most. However, the ring days seemed over for the man who walked gingerly into the parlor wearing a gray sweater over a white shirt and blue tie.

"Mr. Eaton," he said, extending his hand. "Your message is interesting, if not altogether puzzling."

Jake stood half out of respect and half as a reaction to disbelief. Gloria had mentioned that the senator was back in Boston convalescing after an operation, but could this wasted body really be him?

Maybe being operated on, and losing a sister, mounted up. Jake checked the eyes. A fire still burned, but it was dim.

They shook hands. Fowler's grip held the firmness of healthier days. Jake sat back down.

"My brother died years ago," Fowler said, inching up his trousers at the knees and easing himself into a seat.

"So the newspapers said," Jake commented, studying the man across from him. "The important thing is, someone is holding a friend of ours."

Fowler sat emotionless. "And who might that be?" he asked.

"Gloria Gorham."

Fowler tightened his lips. "Gloria?" he repeated softly, glancing at Jake as if he were some mysterious object fallen from the sky. "How do you mean 'holding'?"

"How doesn't matter," Jake said. "What does is that she's being used as bait. In less than three hours, I'm to trade for her return."

"Trade what?"

"Vicki Shaw."

"The writer of the book," Fowler said, as if to himself. "I told Commander Hoenig there might not be a silver lining in this one, but we had to look. You always look if you're in my profession. Try for the positive spin. Politicians can put a positive spin on anything," Fowler said, his eyes brightening.

"Even the deaths of thirteen women?" Jake asked.

Fowler scowled, as if he'd just caught Jake's genuine purpose. "I'm not talking about the Boston Strangler, Mr. Eaton," the senator cautioned. "I'm talking about a manuscript purported to be about that case. It wasn't really. It was more about Bruce Drummond's fantasies. It was his reality, a reality that had no basis in fact."

"You're sure of that?"

"I am," Fowler said, his smile baffling. "I don't see how I can help you, Mr. Eaton. What is it you really want?"

"The truth," Jake said.

Fowler raised his head as if Jake had just challenged him. "Some say a hard commodity to come by in my profession, but my record indicates otherwise." He smiled wistfully. "The people have reelected me more times than I can count. My first campaign was right after DeSalvo was arrested. A tough fight. Nearly lost it."

"Senator—"

Fowler shut Jake out. He leaned back in his seat, his long, bony fingers splayed in front of him, stretching like a cat. "Do you know what keeps this country together? A country as big, as diverse, as complex as ours? I'll tell you: it's a likable politician with a simple idea. But the idea can't be floating out in space or painted on lines on some chart. No. The idea must be demonstrated so the busy shopkeepers can latch onto it, feel comfortable with it." The senator closed his hands, resting them on the arms of his chair. His eyes locked on Jake. "My idea was law and order. Not original, but effective if—*if* I could demonstrate it."

"Albert DeSalvo was your demonstration," Jake said knowingly, "Neil Ebberhardt told me what he did to save his brother."

The senator raised his eyebrows noncommittally. "Back to brothers again, are we? Do you have one?"

Jake nodded.

"Do you get along?" Fowler asked.

"We did," Jake said. "He's dead. The kind of dead you verify when the body's there at your feet, lifeless."

Fowler stretched, lifting his shoulders an inch. "Meaning?"

"Meaning your brother could still be alive. Meaning he's out there somewhere, sick, tortured, killing the innocent once again."

Fowler's expression hardened, showing his indignation.

"My guess is," Jake continued, "your attempt to save him from his tormented self started a conspiracy that's lasted all these years. But," Jake threatened, "it won't last another day."

"And why is that?"

"Because nothing will stand in my way of getting Gloria back. Not you, not some crumbling conspiracy. I'll tear it, and you, down if I have to."

Fowler looked scolded as his face flushed red. "I believe you would," he said finally. "Six months ago, such a threat would have scared the hell out of me. But you're looking at a dying man, Eaton. I have little to live for except what doctors tell me is unbearable pain."

"You could die knowing you helped save Gloria," Jake offered, wondering why he hadn't helped the other women. "Why didn't you stop your brother thirty-plus years ago?"

"I did."

"Not until thirteen women were strangled."

"I acted as soon as I found out the truth," Fowler said. "My brother was, and is, very clever."

"Where is he?" Jake asked.

"Believe me," Fowler said genuinely, "if I knew, I would tell you."

Jake wasn't buying the soft voice. "No games, senator," he said. "We haven't the time."

"It isn't a game," Fowler brooded. "It's a bit of revenge on my own part for Jay Brandon's killing my sister. *His* sister. What triggered the violence this time, I don't know. The pills maybe. He never liked taking his medication. All I know for certain is that he strangled Sarah, then escaped the compound."

"And you haven't heard from him?" Jake asked.

"Once," Fowler said, lowering his eyes. "He called the hospital to see how I was. Can you imagine? He called to see how I was."

"Did he say anything else?"

"Just that I shouldn't worry. He would see to it that the manuscript would never hurt us. He said he would kill anyone who had anything to do with it."

Jake erupted. "And you did nothing!"

Fowler's voice jumped a notch. "I was in the hospital plugged into a thousand tubes. I wasn't even sure I hadn't imagined the call under the influence of all those drugs. Besides," he countered, "the only thing I could do, I did. I requested that Commander Hoenig reopen an internal investigation into the case."

"So the cops could chase their tails around?" Jake said bitterly. "They've been through all those records and have found nothing. Never have."

"Because I didn't follow through," the senator admitted. "In the hospital I kept thinking how much pain we humans can endure. It is phenomenal when you consider it. And none more than the pain we collect in our hearts."

With great effort, Fowler stood. "I kept records, Mr. Eaton. If anyone ever suspected who was behind the conspiracy of silence, these records of each person's involvement would be my protection," Fowler said, stopping in front of a slanted-front desk.

The senator opened the wooden face and took out a full manila folder. He carried it back to Jake and handed it to him. "My brother's guilt is documented in there as well. Jay Brandon would do anything to have what you hold in your hands. He might even give you back Gloria." Fowler sat back down. "It is my hope that he will," he said, wringing his thin fingers. "It won't bring back Sarah, but . . . well, we can hope. There is always hope."

Chapter 31

Vicki Shaw waited near the stone arch across from Harvard Square's Out of Town News kiosk. Jake braked to a quick stop, letting in Vicki and Watson. He jammed the car back into first gear before telling Vicki about Jay Brandon.

The color drained from Vicki's complexion. "He murdered his own sister?" she said, aghast. "What kind of monster is this?"

"The worst kind," Jake said. "Instead of randomly selecting his victims as he did years ago, now he has a purpose: to kill anyone who's come in contact with the manuscript that you and Drum were writing."

Vicki's expression revealed her amazement. "But his *own* sister? What did she have to do with any of this?"

Jake gunned the Saab around slower traffic. "Drummond spoke to Senator Fowler about your book. It wouldn't be a stretch for him to have called the house in Maine. Maybe Drum gave that job to Lori Churchwell. The point is, somehow, Jay Brandon found out about that manuscript and went haywire."

"As he'd done in the past," Vicki added, looking over at Jake. "I found two references in Ruth Hill's files to Sarah Fowler traveling out of state. A strangling occurred both times near the compound. Because they were years apart, in both instances the local authorities wrote them off as random, unrelated acts."

"I guess that explains why Sarah Fowler kept out of the limelight. She spent her entire life taking care of Jay Brandon, keeping him out of sight," Jake said as his car phone rang.

He picked it up, holding the receiver firmly. "This is Jake," he said. He listened as the big man gave an address.

It was 28 Commonwealth Avenue.

Back in his Martin Street apartment, Jake took from a shelf a box of flat-headed shells. Flat-heads were deadly at close range, inaccurate past twenty yards. They were perfect for the short range inside a town house, perfect for one shot. Jake feared that's all he might get.

Jake slipped the last shell into the Magnum's cylinder, closed it, then stood. He picked up Vicki's nylon satchel from his desk, put the folder that Conrad Fowler had given him inside the satchel, adjusted the contents, and zipped it closed.

Vicki waited at the door, Watson standing vigilantly beside her. Vicki was aging by the minute.

"Ready?" Jake asked.

"Is anybody ever?" Vicki said, the tension choking her.

"You'll be fine."

"Why don't I believe that?"

Jake made one last, quick check around, patted Watson encouragingly, then without another word opened the door.

The trip to the town house was like a drive in a funeral procession; the air was hard to come by, the mood solemn. Jake left Vicki with her own thoughts while he played out in his mind how he wanted to proceed. Not that he was making the rules, but in every situation he would have options. What he would not have was time to weigh them, so a plan, a blueprint of action, would help.

He checked his watch. It was five minutes to six when he pulled up to 28 Commonwealth Avenue. He parked in front of the fire hydrant and shut off the engine. He left the keys in the ignition.

"Do you know how to drive a stick shift?" he asked Vicki, this part of his plan clearest of all.

Vicki looked puzzled. "Yes, but . . ."

Jake pointed to the front door of Gloria's town house. "If a man comes out of there and it isn't me," Jake said, "make this call." He handed Vicki a piece of paper with Tommy Dane's number on it. "Tell him I'm in trouble, then get the hell out of here as fast as you can."

Jake reached for the satchel in Vicki's lap. She stopped him with her hand for the briefest of moments. Jake recognized the gesture, the grateful look in her wide eyes.

"I don't plan on you making that call," he said, jerking the bag from her lap, getting out, and closing the door. He let Watson out of the back and headed for the house.

A mound of sand lay in the front yard, a portable cement mixer near it. Jake pulled the Magnum, holding it loosely in his right hand. With Watson beside him, he climbed the granite steps.

Jake pushed the door open and Watson snaked in. Jake followed, adjusting his eyes to the dark shapes before him: a stack of sheetrock, piles of wooden studs, wire tendrils looping down from opened ceilings. Light spilled through a door at the far end of the first floor where the kitchen had been roughed in.

With a hand signal, Jake caught Watson's attention. He wanted the eager dog to move ahead, but slowly. Jake stepped right, then toward the light, his eyes darting about in search of the slightest movement.

What came first was the voice. "You seem to be missing something," the big man said. "Where's Vicki Shaw?"

"Outside."

"Get her."

"When I'm sure Gloria's okay," Jake said, holding his ground.

"She's better than okay," the big man jeered, thrusting Gloria into the doorway. Her blouse was torn open, hanging from her. "She's real fine," he said, yanking her back.

Jake heard his own quick breathing and forced himself to ratchet down his emotions. "I'm not just a delivery boy," Jake shouted. "I'm here to trade."

"You're here to do what I say," the big man said. "Bring me Vicki Shaw!"

Jake lifted the satchel. "Inside this," he said, watching the circling Watson stay hidden in the shadows, "is your way out, Jay Brandon. Your *only* way out."

For the first time, the big man made himself visible. He stood tall in the doorway, his large head thrown forward, his square chin jutting out. "What did you call me?" he asked, pointing in Jake's direction with the semiautomatic pistol he held in his right hand. "I could shoot you right now. You know that."

"I know that, Jay," Jake said, taking his measure of the man twenty feet in front of him. Jake guessed him to be in his early sixties. He wore a rust-colored flannel shirt and khaki trousers with a crease. His thick brown hair looked matted down like windblown wheat. There was an air of apprehension around him, an edge of unpredictability. The unpredictable made Jake nervous.

Jay Brandon shifted his feet. "How'd you know?" he said. "How?"

"Your brother told me." Again Jake motioned with the satchel. "Conrad gave me the records he kept all these years, Jay. Inside here is your freedom. Let Gloria walk out, and it's yours."

Jay Brandon grinned at the humor.

Jake took another step closer. "What's so funny?" he asked.

"You." Jay Brandon was chuckling now. "You're in no position to ask anything." As quickly as it came, the smile left Jay Brandon's face. "Besides, my brother would never do what you say. Never!"

"Things change, Jay."

"Jay Brandon's dead!" The big man's voice echoed in the house. The gun was jerking in his hand. "All right," he spit out. "Here's how it goes. You hold that bag with both hands and walk it over. I want to see what's inside."

"Fine," Jake said. "Gloria for the contents. Vicki Shaw's a bonus."

"Just remember who's in charge, Eaton. Now, move it."

Five feet from the kitchen door, Jake stopped. The big man stepped out, bringing Gloria with him. "Hold that bag away from your body. Stiff arms. If they move, you're dead," he ordered, then searched Jake for a weapon. The Magnum stuck out like a small cannon. The big man tossed it away, pleased with himself. "I told you I knew all the tricks," Jay Brandon teased.

Gloria stood rigidly as if at her own execution.

"Are you all right?" Jake asked her, his arms tiring from holding the nylon bag out in front of him.

"She's fine," Jay Brandon boomed, his face tightening maniacally.

Jake lowered the satchel a fraction, causing Jay to whip his gun toward Gloria.

"If your arms drop without my saying so," Jay warned, "she goes down in a bloody heap. Understand?"

Jake raised the satchel, his muscles stinging.

Jay Brandon waited almost a minute, his cruel gaze going from Jake to Gloria, then back to Jake. "You may lower the satchel now," he said finally.

Jake did gladly, his arms on fire.

"Let's see what's inside," the big man said, pointing his weapon in Jake's direction. "If it's not what it's supposed to be—"

"It is," Jake said. "I packed it myself." Jake eased the satchel forward, slowly maneuvering his right hand under the flap. When Jay Brandon Fowler pulled the nylon bag to him, he found himself looking into the barrel of Jake's .38. "Get down!" Jake yelled at Gloria as two shots from Jay Brandon's gun slammed into the back wall.

As quickly as the shots rang out, Watson was in the air, covering the ten feet between him and Jay Brandon before the man got off another round. Watson's teeth sank into the man's bare flesh just above the wrist. Watson thrashed left and right, tearing open the skin. The big man closed his free hand and swung mightily at the dog's side. The heavy blow only made Watson bite harder, deeper. Jay Brandon fell to his knees, crying out in great, painful sobs. His weapon fell, skittering across the floor in front of him.

Jake kicked the gun out of reach, then helped the shaken Gloria to her feet. She was unable to get a word out, unable to take her terrified eyes off Watson. The wonderful dog was doing all the horrible things she'd thought of doing to Jay Brandon Fowler.

When she no longer cared to look, she noticed Jake's gaze on her. She looked up at him wearily, fondly. He put his arms around her, holding her close. Watson's reckless snarls mixed with the pleas of Jay Brandon pulsing behind them.

"Watson might kill him," she said, as if stating the day of the week. "Jake?"

Jake turned to look. Jay Brandon Fowler was curled on his side, arms held protectively over his face. His cries for help came muffled through tears and his own personal terror as Watson snarled relentlessly inches from the man's stricken face.

Jake turned back to Gloria.

"What are you thinking?" she asked.

"I'm thinking about Drummond," he said, his face gone gray.

"It must have been horrible for him."

"Just what I was thinking."

"But you can't . . . we can't . . ."

Jake looked away, his eyes settling on the grand sweep of the walnut staircase. "You're going to have a wonderful place once the mess is cleaned up."

"Call off Watson, Jake."

Jake nodded, the motion loaded with irritated reluctance. He called Watson to him just as a crack of light in the front of the house caught his eye. It was Vicki Shaw opening the door.

Jay Brandon must have seen it, too. And opportunity. In one painful yet quick scramble, he had his automatic in his hand.

Jake raised his .38. "Don't" was his only warning.

Jay Brandon didn't heed it.

The shot of the hollow point rang through the empty house like a canyon echo.

Finally, after all these years, the Boston Strangler lay dead.

Chapter 32

The private funeral service for Senator Conrad Fowler was held at his summer compound on the Maine island of Vinalhaven late in November. Burial was on the property in the family cemetery, where one month before Jay Brandon Fowler was laid to rest. His thirty-plus-year-old gravestone was covered with gray-green lichen. Carved in the granite were the words: "Died valiantly attempting to save his family." Something similar could have been written for Conrad, who devised his conspiracy of silence to save his family's reputation as well as his career.

As Jake discovered when he read the document Conrad had given him, Conrad was not going to give up a promising career because of the tragic failings of his brother. But neither was he going to submit his brother to the cruelty of prison. Not when Conrad—as attorney general—had indicted many of the prisoners. Jay Brandon, Conrad reasoned, would likely not last one week behind bars.

The conspiratorial ball began rolling when Jay Brandon's wife and children died horribly in a boating accident near the family's Maine summer home. The cold waters running through the channel known as the Fox Island Thorofare were famous for raging current sweeping away all things afloat. Conrad hoped it swept fast enough to lose his brother's criminal past. He announced with anguish his brother's death and the lack of success in finding his body.

"That's the part I never quite understood," Gloria said, sipping champagne in the second-floor bar of Symphony Hall. They had twenty minutes before music director Seiji Ozawa unleashed his baton on Shostakovich. "I know that DeSalvo confessed because he was being paid to, but what good was money to him in prison?"

"None." Jake rotated his cocktail glass on the white tablecloth. "But his wife and two children were free. Keep in mind, Albert broke into houses and stole because he always needed money. In an odd way, going to prison was the path to success that he always hoped for. It made him a rich man, and a proud father when the money was delivered to his wife and children in Germany."

"Courtesy of Michael Reardon," Gloria said knowingly.

"That's right," Jake said. "Reardon was the delivery boy."

"But," Gloria asked, "how did anyone know Michael would do it?"

"That's where Ellison Kitter came in. He was an expert in what motivated people. He could find someone who would do most anything," Jake said. "Remember, Ellison didn't think there had been a conspiracy. He thought DeSalvo was guilty. He sought out the right person for the right task whenever Senator Fowler asked."

"Why?"

"Gratitude for Fowler's support of Ellison's early KSM research."

"So Michael Reardon delivered the money to Albert's wife?"

Jake nodded. "That's right. He received instructions telling him where to pick up the money. His job was to make sure Mrs. DeSalvo got it. Trouble was, after a few years, Albert wanted to raise the ante. If he didn't get the amount he wanted, he threatened to talk to the press. In fact, he had an interview scheduled with *Life* magazine two days before he was found stabbed to death in prison. To this day, no one has been charged with DeSalvo's murder."

"But you think you know who did it," Gloria said as more of the well-dressed crowd gathered at the bar.

Jake nodded. "I do. Doug Turner," he said, explaining that Ellison Kitter knew that Turner wasn't police academy material. Through Kitter's Standard Measure tests, he also knew that Turner was a fearless, capable killer motivated by the challenge of high risk. "Doug Turner was just what Conrad Fowler needed to silence the one man who could tell the truth: Albert DeSalvo."

Gloria sipped her champagne as if trying to wash away some horrible taste. "What about Turner?" she asked.

"He was killed a few years later in a botched robbery attempt. A Boston Homicide detective brought him down," Jake said.

Gloria's eyebrows rose. "At the request of Ronald Hoenig?"

Jake shrugged. "Apparently not. There's no evidence that Hoenig knew anything about the conspiracy. He was just a tough cop doing a tough job."

"Then he really thought there was a copycat on the loose when the Strangler came back?" Gloria asked.

"So it appears," Jake answered as the lights dimmed, signaling ten minutes until the concert began. "Of course, Conrad Fowler was there promoting the idea, but it seems that Hoenig genuinely believed it."

"As you believed that Jay Brandon had actually raped me."

Jake said nothing, looking at her.

Gloria took his hand in hers. "If he had," she said, "I never would have let you call off Watson."

"I almost didn't," Jake admitted.

The lights flashed again as a reminder. As Jake and Gloria followed the slow-moving crowd to their seats, Jake's thoughts went to Vicki Shaw, who had left Harvard University immediately after the death of Jay Brandon Fowler.

She had decided to abandon her dissertation, instead spending her time finishing the book she and Drummond had started. However, this version would rely heavily on the document supplied by Conrad Fowler. Finally, the truth would come out.

"Ironic as hell," Jake said, taking his seat.

"What is?" Gloria straightened the collar on Jake's turtleneck. "What's ironic as hell?"

"Now that the man behind the conspiracy of silence is dead, he's finally talking."